GRANNIES, GUNS AND GHOSTS

GRANNIES, GUNS AND GHOSTS

LARGE PRINT

MADISON JOHNS

GRANNIES, GUNS AND GHOSTS

Madison Johns

Disclaimer: This is a work of fiction.
Any similarity to persons living or dead (unless explicitly noted) is merely coincidental.

Editing and internal layout by Cohesion Author Services
Proofreader Cindy Tahse
Book Cover by http://www.coverkicks.com

Dedication

Dedicated to the spunky seniors of the world.
In memory of Elsie Becker.

CONTENTS

CHAPTER ONE

I, Agnes Barton, of sound mind and body, promise not to throttle my partner in crime, Eleanor Mason, no matter how much she tries to get a rise out of me. I must have lost my mind when I decided to partner with Eleanor in our new detective agency, Pink Ladies. It seemed like a good idea at the time. Truth be known, she had saved my life. *I wonder if I'll ever hear the last of that?* Oh, who was I fooling? She's the only one I'd want to snoop with. While we are quite the odd couple, we're also a great team. So what if the official paperwork and licenses are out of date? That won't stop us from investigating whatever we have a mind to.

Charter Arms couldn't have made a better pistol than The Pink Lady. What woman wouldn't love a pink, ultra-lightweight .38 Special? It's perfect for women to tote around in their handbags. Not that you would call a carpet bag a handbag, by any means. Some of them are large enough to conceal an arsenal of weapons, if a body had a mind to do such a thing.

Unlike the fictional bounty hunter Stephanie Plum, I like to keep my sidearm handy. Nobody really gives a squat what a person of a certain age had concealed in their bags. I suppose most younger folks think we all knit and do all sorts of creative things. Oh, I have a creative mind all right, but not creative enough to dodge Eleanor. Poor dear wouldn't know what to do without our adventures.

I had taken up residence in a camper of all things, parked in a camp-ground in East Tawas, Michigan, on the tranquil shores of Lake Huron. Lucky for me, I got a larger spot at the camp-ground and I had adjusted to living in a Winnebago. My house had been fire-bombed during our last case. It's not so bad. I get to enjoy the misty lake as the sun rises, and some of the most spectacular sunsets in Michigan.

I eyed my cat, Duchess, and said, "I hope it doesn't take 'til winter for our house to be rebuilt."

Duchess responded with, "Meow."

"I know, girl, no mourning doves here," I said to her. I strode by the mirror as I made my way into the bathroom and deep lines formed as I grimaced. I'm still wearing my pink bathrobe with pink ruffles, white sandals covering my feet. My unruly salt and pepper hair was tangled and I tried to work my fingers through the knots.

Every dang morning it's the same thing. My hair looks like a rooster did it in my sleep. Puffy dark circles were apparent, obviously from the restless slumber as my hip ached something fierce last night.

I made my way into the kitchen and poured coffee grounds into my new, fancy-dancy coffee maker that is supposed to make a good latte. *If I ever figure out how to use the damn thing!* It's only seven in the morning and I'm already cussing, if only in my head at the moment.

I jumped and bumped against the counter and clutched my chest when my door vibrated nearly off the hinges. *Whoever could that be? And this early?*

I pulled back the pink lace curtains to reveal a familiar pair of friendly blue eyes. Eleanor, had her face pressed to the window with both her hands against my door like a lost puppy begging to be let in.

I yanked open the door and watched in amusement as she tried to steady herself, resembling a Weeble Wobble. *What is the saying? Weebles Wobble, but we don't fall down.*

"Have you been camped outside my door all night waiting for me to let you in?" I body blocked the doorway. I wasn't ready to let her in just yet.

She puffed up her chest, trying unsuccessfully to act offended. "Of course not, Agnes. I just didn't want to bother you if your hot-shot lawyer man is here." She giggled, her large belly jiggling. "Unless you want an audience." Her eyes danced.

She wishes.

"Who?"

"You know perfectly well whom I'm talking about. The last time I came here the camper was rockin' so hard that I thought there was an earthquake occurring inside."

"It was earth-shattering." I frowned. "Andrew Hart has gone back to wherever he came from, just as I knew he would."

"Did he say when he's coming back?"

She actually sounded sincere. "I don't know, nor do I care. I'm seventy-two and I don't have the time for the entanglement a man would create in my life." I cared all right, but I'd never let her know it. If I gave it too much thought I'd be no good to anybody. Andrew left, and I wish under better terms, but me being the stubborn woman I am, we left on a sour note. An argument over coffee creamer of all things, and I crossed the line when I insisted he stay in town. But no sense in regrets now. It's too late.

Eleanor interrupted my thoughts. "Yes, you do, or else you wouldn't be acting so moody today."

"I'm not moody!" So much for making pledges to myself; I should have remembered who I was dealing with.

"Maybe I should buy you one of those mood rings and prove it to you."

"That's ridiculous, and you should know it interprets body temperature, not moods."

Eleanor continued on completely ignoring the fact I wasn't playing along. "You'd be black today, I think."

I pushed El aside and closed the door behind me, descended the metal stairs and made my way to the picnic table, fidgeting with the floral arrangement in its center.

Eleanor frowned; she sneaked a peek inside, but joined me at the table.

I caught sight of the burgundy awning swaying in the wind. Although only morning, the distinct scent of smoldering campfires lingered in the cool air. Quiet, solitary campers moved about in neighboring campsites, while others made their way to the showers. Small children stayed close to their mothers with towels thrown over their shoulders.

I watched Eleanor give the exterior of the camper a once over from the table. Her eyes enlarged to the size of saucers, but she kept her tongue for the moment. Her thin hair looked to be styled. She must have been to the hair salon. *I hope I won't be the talk of the town now.* Being a beautician is kind of like being a detective except that people are more than willing to spill their guts. Eleanor had herself poured into a lime green capri and matching tee set. It was a few sizes too small and didn't complement her fair skin, but I won't be the one to say so. She's eighty-two and I know those would be fighting words. She resembles the actress Betty White with plenty of sass.

"Pretty fancy digs if you ask me," Eleanor said.

"I suppose, but I'll be glad when they finish rebuilding my house."

"Why bother? Why not just collect the insurance money and buy a new place? Shucks, at your age, you might not live long enough to even enjoy the place."

"Is there something I should know? Have you hired a hit man to off me?"

She gave me a hard stare. "Who would I annoy then?" she laughed.

"Who indeed?"

I doubted she'd understand why I wanted my house rebuilt. It was taken from me. I didn't have a choice, and dammit, that's my property with the perfect soil and all the steamy memories of Andrew.

Stop it, Agnes.

I met Eleanor's eyes. Her lips curved into a hint of a smile yet her eyes softened. She knew me too well.

"I suppose you'd like to check out the inside?" I asked.

"You betcha." She grinned.

I led the way inside the Winnebago. I poured coffee into two mugs, spilling a generous portion on the floor. Duchess scampered over and proceeded to lap it up. Eleanor gave the interior a careful inspection. Her eyes cut to mine; her mouth gaped open, and her eyes practically bugged out of her head. "Where did you get this camper?"

"Oh, one of those police auctions." Trying to act nonchalant, I said, "I got a real good deal, too." I gazed at the purple walls with hot-pink couches and dinette seats equally adorned. "I wonder why nobody else wanted it." I tried unsuccessfully to hide a snicker.

"Holy moly… it looks like someone threw up purple in here."

She grinned, revealing two holes where teeth used to be. She had them pulled the week before and it was sort of an ongoing joke between us. Eleanor is the perfect target for ill-placed jokes, but I only do it because that's what she would do and has done to me.

I placed my hands on my hips and grinned. "I know, isn't it great?"

"Fits right in with our Pink Lady P.I. agency."

"I hope Elsie Bradford or one of the other social icons in town doesn't find out about this place."

"I'm sure they'll hear about it soon enough.

A little birdie will probably tell them," El said, glancing toward the ceiling.

"I think its name is Eleanor." I wiped up the remaining coffee with a towel. "Maybe little bird isn't the correct word."

Her eyes met mine. "Watch it, Aggie, or I might let it slip about the rockin' camper. The girls were so disappointed you never introduced them to Andrew when he was in town."

I rolled my eyes. "I bet. So, what's up? You have been making yourself scarce lately."

"I was giving you some space." She avoided my gaze, never a good sign when dealing with Eleanor.

"Since when do you leave me room to breathe?"

Eleanor's face turned red. "I do have other interests, you know."

"Like what?" I asked. I had the feeling there was something going on and I was being left out of the loop.

When she spoke, she did so quietly and I barely heard what she said. "What? Speak up. You know I can't hear you when you don't speak up."

"Ghost ship." Her face looked completely serious, deadly serious.

"Ghost ship?" I asked, bursting into a fit of laughter.

El's face screwed up into a sneer. "That's why

I didn't want to tell you. I knew you'd act like this."

"Like what?"

"Agnes Barton, you are the biggest sour-puss sometimes. If you stayed out from under that man long enough you'd know it's the talk of East Tawas."

"You don't have to be so testy, dear. What ghost ship?"

"*Erie Board of Trade*. It's the most exciting thing to happen around here since our last adventure."

Changing the subject, I said, "Andrew's gone now. I guess you'll have to catch me up on all the local gossip."

I heard banging in my bedroom and I made my way there. Duchess leapt into the air doing a half-turn somersault. I then heard a drawer thrown open behind me and metal utensils sailed to the floor. Eleanor had squatted down and the sound of either a fart or rending fabric echoed through the room. She retrieved a pancake turner, jumped up, and swatted at something flying in the air.

I froze. Another damn bee got in. Before I had time to react, Eleanor had turned on the water and picked up the sprayer.

"Don't you dare spray that bee!" I shouted.

Her eyes widened. "If you have another idea you better get at it, because that's the biggest bee I have ever seen."

I raced into the bathroom and brought back a can of hairspray. I removed one sandal and showered the bee with freezing hairspray. "Duck!" I yelled.

Eleanor ran toward the front and hid behind a chair while I waited to move. It took a few more sprays, but the bee dropped to the floor where I was able to smash the bugger. "It works every time," I said with confidence.

"I've missed you, Aggie. Who else can I have this much fun with?" She eyed Duchess. "You'd think that cat of yours would be more help eradicating insects. Does she bring those in too?"

"Actually," I laughed, "Duchess is a notorious bee slayer. Her wanted poster is hanging in every hive in the county."

CHAPTER TWO

I was dressed appropriately for my first outing of the day. With my bathrobe still on, I made my way toward the communal showers with Eleanor in tow. When we walked in the brick building and I saw the crowd ahead of us, a loud sigh escaped my lips. I had to wait like the rest of the campers for the showers, and from the looks of it, I'd be waiting a good while. The tiled floor of the bathroom was layered with sand like a sandstorm had just blown inside, from beach goers no doubt. *Seriously, can't they clean the floor more often?* Not entirely bothered by the inconvenience as of yet, I shrugged in Eleanor's direction. It's not like we had a case yet.

When a tall brunette exited a shower stall, Eleanor stopped a teenager before she entered.

"I don't think so. You don't expect this old woman here to wait any longer, do you?" She pointed toward me. "I mean, what if the poor thing can't stand up that long?" El gave me the eye as if expecting me to play along.

I stood there, and right on cue tried to act feeble enough by leaning to the right on one hip.

"Go ahead, Grandma," the girl giggled, much to the amusement of her friends who all joined her in laughter.

She won't be laughing when she's seventy-two. She'll be crying. Although acting my age had its benefits, such as getting me into the shower sooner.

Eleanor entered the shower with me.

I shot her a look. "Whatever are you doing, Eleanor?"

"I thought we were friends," she pouted.

"Yes, but we don't need to be that close."

Eleanor stomped out, acting like I had offended her. Sometimes I worry about Eleanor. Last I had heard, Mr. Wilson, Eleanor's last *friend*, was sporting a neck cuff. This was under the, 'I don't want to know' category.

I stood under the weak spray that came from the shower head, soaped myself up and washed my hair real quick-like. Lord knows you can't count on the hot water lasting. Sweet memories of my house came back to haunt me; memories of Andrew and the day that he had hopped in my shower with me. I remembered how mad I was at the time. Now I just wished he were here.

No point in regrets now. It's best to just let these thoughts vanish from my mind. *If only that were possible.*

I pulled on my yellow panties and push-up bra. The last thing I needed was to be seen looking like my boobs were heading south, which at my age isn't that much of a stretch. Although just last week at my physical, the girl that did my mammogram complimented me on them. It's a blessing to get any compliment, no matter where it originates. I'm not what you'd call top heavy, unlike Eleanor. I have worn a bra since they were invented, I think. They had made the cups all pointy in those days like you'd see in some damn Madonna video.

I pulled on white shorts, a white tee, and carried my sandals, knowing the beach is where we planned to go next.

When I exited the shower, I decided not to thank the girl next in line. She giggled at me when I passed by, and I felt the urge to trip her but didn't. Younger folks don't get what it's like to be a senior citizen. I hoped I'd live long enough to see this girl grow older. I'll run her over with Eleanor's electric wheelchair like some of my friends do, just for kicks.

Eleanor was waiting outside and followed me back to my Winnebago from a comfortable distance.

Clackety-clack.

We both turned sharply and watched a black camper that swayed and shimmied as it went past. The wood paneled sides resembled —

13

"Damn gypsies," Eleanor muttered. "Or witches."

I turned and gave Eleanor a sharp look. "Are you kidding me? What nonsense is traveling around inside that head of yours, El?"

"Well ... the trailer is black."

"Meaning?"

El's bottom lip appeared, but I moved her along and back to my camping spot. Sure enough, straight across from my Winnebago the black monstrosity of a camper was backing in. Whoever drove the blasted thing must have taken the same driver's course as Eleanor because they almost took out the camper next to them.

"See, Aggie, there is somebody that drives worse than me." She nodded in affirmation.

I grimaced. Now, I know it might seem a bit rude to stare and all, but I couldn't look away.

Finally after a few more tries the camper of sorts parked, but had snagged the clothes line from the neighboring campsite. Multi-colored bathing suits now were strewn across the camper. I heard the engine cut off and the trailer shimmied as footsteps clucked down the steps. The door screeched open and two scrawny legs appeared from the doorway with black pointy-toed shoes.

"El, I think you're right. It's a witch!" I trembled while El hugged me close.

14

"I won't let her get you, Aggie." With that, Eleanor left me and ran into the Winnebago. She slammed the door behind her and, knowing Eleanor the way I did, I'm betting she locked herself inside.

The gypsy trailer's door slammed shut and a woman glared over to where I stood. She had long, black, scrawny hair and wore a black dress. *She did look like a gypsy*, I thought. When I glanced at the trailer, I noticed the fabric that hung down nearly covering the windshield. No wonder the woman parked like she did.

The woman walked toward me and stopped just where the driveway pavement started on her side.

"Why you stare so? You no see a Romanian before?" She stomped her foot for emphasis.

I shook my head in response as a large dog I hadn't even noticed came bounding toward me. It was one of those hellhounds, I think.

I couldn't move and held my breath, shutting my eyes. I went to trembling and my teeth were nearly chattering in fright. I could almost feel the hellhound's breath upon me!

"HISSSSSSSS!"

I snapped open my eyes. Duchess stood at the ready, her gray back arched in perfect *cat whipping dog's ass* mode. She must have gotten out when Eleanor ran inside.

15

Now for some dang reason, not only did that dang hellhound stop, he turned about and yelped in his retreat.

"Huh?" I spoke aloud. "That hellhound is afraid of cats?" I said to Duchess.

She looked up at me and I swear she smiled. Duchess ran to me, and I scooped her up and gave her a good scratch under the chin, as she liked so much. I was so grateful she had saved my life that I promised to give her an ample amount of catnip later.

"Quit looking at me, you old crone," the woman said. "Leotyne Williams will—"

I didn't stick around to listen to more of what she had to say. Truth be known, I didn't want to know. I rattled the door to the Winnebago until Eleanor opened the door.

I ambled inside and sat down on the couch and exhaled so loud you'd have thought a whirlwind was inside.

"Thanks, El. What a pal you are," I finally said in exasperation.

"W-well I-I th-thought you came inside with me." Her eyes fixed on the stove, apparently willing to look anywhere except directly in my eyes.

I gasped. "You know dang well I didn't. You deserted me," I huffed. "I was almost killed out there by a hellhound." I waved my arms about in the biggest display of body language I could muster.

Eleanor chewed her fingernail. "Hellhound?" She giggled. "Really, Aggie?"

I wanted to choke Eleanor.

"Oh, God, please don't let me go to jail for killing Eleanor."

She chuckled at that. "Aggie, if you were in that much danger, how come you're not dead?"

"Because Duchess saved me, if you need to know."

"Hellhounds are afraid of a cat? That's rich, Aggie," she smirked.

My eyes widened. "I think she was about to put a curse on me. I think you're right, she's a gypsy."

"Did she mention her name or were you too busy crapping yourself?"

"Leotyne something." I moved to pour a cup of coffee and popped it into the microwave to reheat it.

The microwave dinged. "A potential client called while you were outside battling hellhounds," Eleanor said.

I whirled around. "Really? What did they say?"

"She sounded kinda upset really. We might want to hightail it over to the Butler Mansion right quick. There has been a murder. The woman was quite insistent on the phone that we come before they go hauling off the body."

I stared at her thinking about the last time we'd been on a case. It revolved around Robinson's Manor, a bed and breakfast where in 1968 an entire family was murdered, a cold case that El and I had solved by default a few months ago.

I drank down my brew fast-like and we ambled out the door and into Eleanor's Caddy that was parked nearby.

Chapter Three

I screwed up my face. "Butler Mansion, El?"
"You remember about the Butlers, don't you?
Clarence Butler was in the shipping business. He
did quite well for himself and built a three-story
mansion north of East Tawas."

"I haven't lived here as long as you, El."

"Well, to listen to yourself talk you certainly
act as you have."

I merged onto US 23 which was busy like
always, but it seemed even more so today.

"I wonder why it's so busy today, El. It's not
even the weekend."

She clucked her tongue. "I told you there
has been a ghost ship spotted on Lake Huron."
She continued before I could get a word in. "It
appears on the lake when it's foggy."

"Seriously? A ghost ship?" I acted interested
even though I doubted the validity of her claims.

She coughed. "I tried telling you that before.
It's the *Erie Board of Trade* or so the story goes."

"Tell me more, Eleanor, as this is oh so
interesting," I mocked her.

Eleanor screwed up her face with menacing intent. "They say that the Captain sent a crewman up to the lookout chair during a storm and he fell to his death!"

"Really? You mean this is kinda like an urban legend?"

She continued on with her story. "Later, they spotted the ghostly figure of the crew member in different areas of the ship. When they came to port, the crew told the eerie tale and when they went back out onto the Lake Huron the next day," Eleanor clapped her hands with a resounding slap, "the ship sank! Never to be seen again."

"Except as a ghost ship?" I asked.

"Yes. She sank in 1883."

I shook my head, always a doubting Thomas. "That sounds believable," I chuckled. "I hope they didn't bring Blackbeard the Pirate with them." I continued to laugh. "I bet their sister ship was the *Flying Dutchman*."

"Keep laughing all you want. Just wait until you see it and you'll change your tune real quick."

"St-Stop it, El. You're gonna make me pee my pants."

I passed a car. "Whoever saw the ghost ship must have better eyesight than I do because I can't see a dang thing when the lake is foggy."

"Humph." El turned to look out the window, sneaking a peek in my direction. "You'll see it soon enough and when you do, I'm gonna tell you I told you so!"

I drove down the road that led to the Butler Mansion and a chill crept through me. *Damn El and all her ghost ship talk!*

"What are you shivering for, Aggie? I thought you didn't believe in ghosts."

"Nope, sure don't. Unless I meet one first hand that is."

"You are just swinging the pendulum in your direction now, Aggie."

I rolled my eyes. Following Eleanor's directions, I drove up a drive that led to a well-manicured lawn of the Butler Mansion. I braked hard as I saw a group of seniors surrounding a man lying on the ground.

I narrowed my eyes. "They called us before the sheriff or the state police?"

"Yup, I told them to wait a spell," El said.

"You do know that this is potentially a crime scene, right? The law should be here before everybody else is called."

Eleanor fidgeted with her fingers. "They'll shoo everyone off and we'll never get to find out what happened. It's not my fault folks trust us more than that lame-brained sheriff."

I didn't much care for Sheriff Peterson myself, but I do have some respect for law enforcement. Of course, I much preferred Trooper Sales to him, but it didn't matter who I liked or didn't like. I need to be a law-abiding citizen, and that means securing the crime scene at this point.

El and I got out real quick and approached the hysterical crowd.

"Oh, my God, my poor husband is dead!" a woman's voice wailed. It belonged to a fiery redhead poured into a tight, strumpet-red dress, her breasts nearly popping out. "I can't b-believe this. Oh, God, why did you have to take my husband on our wedding day?"

"Wedding day!" Eleanor shouted and shuffled her feet as the woman turned to look at her.

"I'm Agnes Baron,, P.I. and this here is my assistant, Watson." I thumbed in El's direction.

El's eyes narrowed. "That's fine. Watson is way smarter than Sherlock Holmes ever was."

"Have you ever read Sherlock Holmes, dear? If you had ... oh forget it. We're here to investigate."

"Are you Miss Marple?" a woman dressed in a maid uniform asked me inquisitively.

I smoothed my hair back. "I fancy myself more of a Jessica Fletcher."

"She's such a know-it-all, Aggie. You don't want to be her," Eleanor laughed.

"I'm certainly not trying to be Miss Marple or any other fictional character. I'm the real deal." I took an elegant stance like I was posing for a magazine. "I have never even read an Agatha Christie book before," I insisted.

I walked toward the body, knelt to check for a pulse, but found none. I glanced at an open window on the third floor, and then back at the maid. "How long has he been laying out here?"

"Thing is," the redhead started, "we're just not sure. You see, we moved here yesterday and —"

"I thought you just were muttering that this was your wedding day."

"I heard her too, Aggie," Eleanor affirmed with a bob of her head.

The woman's eyes shifted slightly. "Like I was saying, if you'd quit interrupting me. We were married yesterday and had a reception celebrating the event late into the night," she giggled. "Of course, we did manage to consummate our marriage."

"Why would I think anything else?" I asked.

Red glared at me, but continued. "He left momentarily and —"

"Needed to take another Viagra," Eleanor slipped in.

"Point is, I must have fallen asleep, and when I awoke this morning, I realized he was missing. We then tore the place apart looking for him." She started bawling something awful now.

"What did you say your name was?" I asked. It had occurred to me that I should tell somebody to call the sheriff's department, but I wanted the rest of this woman's story.

23

"I didn't," the woman snapped. "My name is Betty Lou Butler, but don't you dare call me just plain Betty ever."

"Okay, Betty. And your husband's name is?"

She glared at me and tightened her lips, not saying a word. I had struck a nerve.

"His name was Herman," the maid said. "Herman Butler." She nodded. "I'm Teresa." The maid shook my hand vigorously. "I knew right away that I should call you." She smiled just then. "I know you can find out what really happened to Mr. Butler." Her black uniform with a ruffled white collar flapped in the wind. Her round cheeks blushed slightly in a show of a possible sunburn. I guessed her to be about thirty.

"And Herman just moved here. Is that right?"

"He just inherited the house since the latest Butler died unexpectedly a few months past," the maid said.

"I see. And how did the last Butler die?"

"Hunting accident."

"I see. Herman inherited the house and got married to this Betty Lou and now he's dead."

"Yes, quite," the maid replied.

"Gee, these Butlers sure are accident prone," El said. "Presuming he fell out the window up there," she observed.

Betty Lou pushed the maid aside. "I don't know what you're implying here, but I had nothing to do with—"

24

El interrupted her with, "Marrying a guy and then him kicking the bucket soon after?"

"And after he just inherited a mansion. Quite coincidental if you ask me," I added.

I stared at the body that was face down on the lawn. My eyes drifted upward toward the open window on the third floor again. It was a tiny window, though; too tiny for this man to squeeze through, or so it seemed.

Herman's arms were both bent at the elbows and his legs were at an odd angle.

"His legs look broken," Eleanor observed.

I nodded. "Somebody call the sheriff's department and please move away from the body."

"It was just an accident," Betty Lou said. "He must have gotten confused last night and fell out the window is all."

"So now he was confused?" I countered. "But not too confused to get married just yesterday?"

"I just know that I didn't have nothing to do with this, and when the sheriff shows up he'll tell you so."

"Will he now?" I couldn't help but stare at that open upstairs window. "Mind if I go inside?"

Betty Lou huffed in the background and pulled a pack of cigarettes from her cleavage, complete with lighter, and lit up while we made our way toward the house.

CHAPTER FOUR

El and I maneuvered the few steps that led inside the Butler Mansion, goosebumps immediately appearing on my arms. I shrugged it off. *Too much ghost talk from Eleanor.* I brushed the thought away and focused on doing a good once -before the sheriff and state police showed up like a bat outta hell.

"You know, El, the thought that a murder might just have happened here... is a bit unnerving." I laughed nervously.

"Why, a person would be wacky if they didn't feel that way," El replied.

Inside was a drawing room. I think that was what rich folks called it. The walls were covered with textured eggshell-white wallpaper that looked quite lovely. There was also a white stone fireplace along one wall, quite ornamental. It was complete with carvings of ghastly figures, but I didn't want to say anything that would sound impolite. On the mantle above was a series of urns. I shudder to think that they contained ashes, but as curious as I was, I had to ask the maid who followed us inside. "I sure hope there aren't any ashes in those urns."

"Oh, my," Eleanor wheezed.

The maid laughed. "No, they're just for decoration. Most of the Butler descendants were buried up on the hill at the back of the property."

"Cemetery?" Eleanor exclaimed, grabbing my arm in a tight grasp, her fingernails cutting into the flesh of my arm.

"It's a family cemetery, to be exact. All the Butler descendants were buried up there." She hushed up just then like she wanted to say more but thought better of it. Her eyes cut to the door.

"If you could direct us upstairs, I'd sure love to have a look at that room. You know, the one that Herman might have fallen from."

Just then, a breeze blew the hair at the nape of my neck and I turned. Sheriff Peterson's frame had filled the doorway, his hair and tan uniform clinging to his bulky body, as unfit as ever. He stood there for a moment, possibly attempting to regain his composure. We were not what you'd call friends or even allies.

"What are you doing here?" he bellowed, ejecting spittle from his large mouth. "I can't imagine who might have called you down here."

I stood quite erect and said, "Then don't ask."

"Yup, don't ask the questions if you can't

handle the truth," Eleanor piped in. Her fingers picking nervously at her shirt as Peterson stared at her. She then shrugged. "I told Aggie it was a bad idea."

"You what?"

"Oh, come on, Aggie. You know we should have called in the guns sooner."

The sheriff motioned us outside with a thumb. "Out, ladies. And I'm using the word *ladies* lightly."

El gasped and I just glared at the man, wishing for another election sooner rather than later, but we walked outside where the state police and an ambulance waited. Trooper Sales was in fine form, his slim body poured into his slick blue Michigan State Police attire. *If only I was five years younger.* I can't help such thoughts, but I was married to a trooper, after all. I had been a widow for thirty-plus years now.

Sales was standing next to Betty Lou, who was bawling again. "My poor husband is dead and on our wedding day."

"We heard that part before," I said.

"Well, they haven't, Mrs. Snoopy pants." Betty Lou's cheeks turned fire-engine red. She turned back to the trooper. "I believe something supernatural is at hand." She nodded profusely. "This house is haunted and I believe," she paused, pounding her chest, "that a ghost killed my husband, pushed him out that window." She pointed upward to the third floor window.

That sure got everybody's attention. "Ghost?" I laughed.

"Yes. Ever since we came to town we have heard strange noises and sounds. I even saw a ghostly apparition on one occasion."

"That's a bit hard to swallow," I said.

I could see from the facial expressions of the sheriff and trooper that for once we might be in agreement.

"I hate to agree with you, Aggie," Peterson said, "but that is more than a mouthful of nonsense."

Sales' facial expression remained stoic. "Ghosts are not real. Those ghost hunter shows have folks all in an uproar over nothing. Way too much hype these days."

I listened in silence until Sales and Peterson finished asking Betty Lou all the same questions I had.

"So, we have a dead guy who happened to just inherit this mansion, and a brand new bride," I said. "Did any of your guests hear anything last night?"

"I'm sure they did," Betty Lou replied suggestively.

I pursed my lips. "Was that before or after your husband fell to his death?"

Betty Lou folded her arms tightly. "I told you that when you showed up here unannounced."

"We are here in regards to a case," I reminded her.

"We received a strange phone call, I hope not from the ghost." Eleanor bit her finger.

"There has also been a ghost ship reported in the area," Betty Lou reaffirmed. "It might be related."

"Thank you, ladies for your input," Trooper Sales finally cut in. "We'll take it from here."

"What? I'm on a case here."

"*We* are," Eleanor reminded me. "This isn't a one woman operation here, Aggie."

"It's also a crime scene," Trooper Sales reminded me. "It's best if you two move on out. We can handle it from here."

"That's not fair," Eleanor pouted. "Tell them they can't do that, Aggie!"

"Actually, I think they can. They're the law remember."

"I know you two are gonna dig up clues like you always do, but crime scenes are off limits, hear?" Sales said. "You're not just jeopardizing the crime scene but the investigation as well."

"I believe it was already compromised," I informed him. "There was a whole group of seniors gawking at the body when we got here."

"Like who?" Sales looked around.

"They must have left when you showed up."

"Aggie, there wasn't anyone here when we showed up, dear. Just the actress and the maid."

31

I stomped my way back to the Caddy and as I whirled back for one last glance, the upstairs window was closed! I gulped. *That just couldn't be!* We made our way back into Tawas and the campground. "Are you sure there wasn't anyone but the widow and the maid when we arrived?"

"I'm sure. Why?"

"I could have sworn I saw a group of people standing over the body, and the upstairs window was open then closed when we left."

"That place is haunted, for sure." El hugged herself.

I'd have told her she was crazy just then, but I knew what I saw. "I'm not a confused senior here."

"Where did that come from, Aggie?"

Ignoring El's comment, I said, "We'll have to head back to that house when the law leaves. I wish we'd had more time before Peterson and company showed up."

"I see you two still don't see eye-to-eye."

"You'd think he would have changed his tune, but it's the same old song."

CHAPTER FIVE

El and I had a leisurely lunch of turkey on wheat with a generous smidgen of Miracle Whip for flavor. We were sipping our sun tea that took about all the ice I had to make it cold. I had left it outside for an equivalent of three days. It was a might strong, but I needed the caffeine.

"We really need to get back to the Butler Mansion," I said. "It really burns me that the sheriff showed up so soon."

"How are we gonna do that, Aggie? Won't they have like crime scene tape keeping the place locked up?"

"Not necessarily. I killed a man before, remember? They only do that in the movies unless it's a real bad scene like a serial killer."

"That was different, dear. That was a home invasion. It was self-defense," El said with honesty. "Although I can't imagine what with a widow and staff that live at the Butler Mansion that they'll be able to lock the place up."

"Highly unlikely. So what did you think of the widow in question?"

"Drama queen."

"Besides that. Do you think she has what it takes to haul a drunk man up to the third floor and shove him out some tiny window?"

"Oh, I'm not sure, Aggie, but she was playing up the accident scenario to the hilt."

"Right up to the point when she started blaming ghosts."

El winked. "That sure shot her credibility right out the window." El sipped more tea before continuing. "Although I do believe she may be right."

I hastily stood, hands on hips. "And what about, I'd like to know."

"There might really be ghosts haunting the Butler Mansion. It was built in the 1880's."

"That doesn't mean anything. You people in this town have gone plain loco. Ghosts and ghost ships my pa-tutee!"

Just then a crowd of seniors scampered through the campground making their way toward the beach. I wouldn't say they were moving at the fastest gait, many using canes and walkers.

"I sure hope they are not walking toward the light," I said.

"Me, either. That would be half the town I think."

Walking toward the light was one of those age-related things us seniors think about, but are not ready to do. Least of all me.

"We might as well see what all the hoopla is about."

"You're right, Aggie. I'd hate to miss out on any fun."

"Or trouble."

"You're hardly one to talk, Aggie. I can recall quite a few instances of Aggie behaving badly."

I glared at her as we walked. My eyes met those of the new gypsy that rolled into camp today. She had a stance about her that was eerie at best. Just as we passed, she pointed her boney finger my way. "The devil will see you soon!" she screeched at me. I quickened my pace, and I'm afraid to say, I left Eleanor in my dust.

"Aggie, would you hold up for a minute?"

I waited until she joined me and then I went to babbling. "Did you hear what that gypsy said?"

"She's just trying to rattle you, dear."

I was nearly crying by now. "She said 'the devil will see me soon'. What do you think she meant?" Stars danced about my head and I felt woozy. El, always the consummate friend that she was, said, "Maybe you are. I mean you haven't been to church in quite some time and you were consorting with that lawyer man."

"What about Mr. Wilson and you?"

"It's not about me, it's about you, Aggie. Do you think that ole gypsy has the sight? She could very well see into the future." Eleanor rubbed her hands together. "Just maybe she can give me some stock tips."

"Maybe I can just tip you over."

"See, that's why you're gonna meet the devil before me." Eleanor was belly laughing now. Her face was so red I thought she was having an attack of some sort, until the snorts that is.

I stomped away. "I'd never joke about it if a gypsy put a curse on you."

"Okay, so you don't believe in ghosts but you believe in curses and witches?"

"I'm not talking to you right now."

"What did you do to cause that gypsy to get so peeved at you?"

I whirled around and faced her. "I didn't do anything. Her hellhound nearly killed me and you're making jokes at my expense."

"Really, Aggie, are you that concerned about that old gypsy?"

"Yes!"

"We'll just have to figure out a way to get her to leave real quick-like."

I rolled my eyes. "I don't want any part of this. I have enough problems already."

"Oh, what now?"

"For one, we don't know for sure we have a case. The maid didn't exactly hire us. And with my P.I License not exactly active... "

"So, when has that ever stopped us?"

"A cash flow would be nice, you know. We might want to go to Florida this winter."

"Now you're talking, toots."

We continued into the beach area and it was packed. I mean packed with seniors, packing who knows what. They each had a camera in their hands and black, ugly sunglasses, the kind that go over your glasses. For the most part, seniors are very light-sensitive.

Elsie Bradford was even here. I made my way toward where she was perched on a sturdy wood chair dressed in her usual powder blue pants with matching long sleeved shirt. Her hair was styled as per her bi-weekly hair salon appointment. She also happens to be the queen peacock of the social circles here in East Tawas, and quite happy with her status, I might add. Seated right next to her, also on wooden chairs, were Bill and Marjory Hays, dressed alike in mustard yellow.

"Hello, Elsie," I greeted her. "Fancy meeting you at the beach."

Her eyes widened. "What with the ghost ship and all, where else would I be?"

I smiled. "What is all this talk of a ghost ship lately?"

"It's the *Erie Board of Trade* ,they say. I haven't seen it yet, but I'm quite hopeful, quite."

"Hmm, so who actually did see it?"

"Doubting Thomas, are you, dear?" Elsie

smiled. "Did you hear my sister is in town, gonna stay the summer?"

"No, I hadn't heard that one," I said between gritted teeth, shooting Eleanor a look that could kill. "El, dear why didn't you mention that Elsie's, uhm, sister was here?"

"Well, now, if it's not Agnes Barton. And after all these years," Mildred said. Her wide mouth was twisted into a snarl. Her tightly-curled hair was gray with a few strands of black intermixed. She wore a purple polyester dress that looked like it was ripped from the sixties.

I turned and ignored her with the best of intentions. *I wonder how fast I can run off the sand before Mildred goes into rage mode.* I whirled just in time to take an opened-palmed slap to my face. I fell to the sand with a thump, spraying sand in my eyes while Eleanor went in motion and tackled Mildred in one swoop.

"Oww ... hey ... yowza!" the woman screamed.

"El, get off that battle axe before you hurt yourself."

"Battle axe?" Elsie exclaimed. "Why, I never!"

"I'm sure you have as there was proof in the form of a child." I kinda wished I'd bitten my tongue off. I hadn't planned to squabble with Elsie over her sister, Mildred Winfree.

Never trust anyone with the name of Mildred. I've met more than a few and they're all bat-shit crazy. Go plain nuts on you if they think you even looked cross-eyed at them. If you talk to their man, they go postal. That pretty much sums up Mildred and me to a tee. I talked to her then husband Charles. Okay so we might have done the nasty, but in my defense I hadn't known he was married to crazy ole Mildred at the time. When I found out, I was as shocked as she was. Now, that was twenty years ago, but from the slap she planted on me, obviously she hadn't forgotten.

Eleanor and Mildred finally parted and both sat on the beach, panting heavily. That's about how most senior fights go—more than a minute and it's time for a nap.

I helped Eleanor up and well out of Mildred's reach. El had a nasty scratch across her arm and I held my hand over it to staunch the flow of blood.

"I don't have an issue with you, Elsie, but really, you need to get a handle on your sister."

Mildred jumped at me again, but I moved clear and she fell face first on the beach, taking enough sand in her mouth to cause her to cough and sputter. I just guided El out of harm's way, through the campground, and back into her Caddy. I drove toward the hospital.

"I don't need no dang hospital," Eleanor sputtered.

She held a hand over her arm that was still

bleeding. "Lacerations are nothing to mess with, El, and neither are skin tears."

"Mildred is such a dirty fighter. Who knew she'd go after you like that, Aggie."

"I know. She didn't even give me a chance to react," I laughed. "It's been so many years, and just my luck, dementia hasn't set in."

"If she has memory loss, I bet it's just short term."

I nodded. "It wasn't really my fault, you know ... I mean her husband. It was just an accident."

"Yup, you accidentally fell right on him, eh, Aggie?"

"That's not," I pulled my shirt from my neck, as it felt tight, "how it happened, exactly."

I could feel El's eyes on me. "How exactly did it happen?"

"Oh, El, I don't want to bore you with the details. Let me just say that Charles was quite the dancer back in the day and danced me right outta my clothes. I had no idea he was married."

"Or married to bat-crazy Mildred."

"Nope, and we have been arch-enemies ever since. Not my choice, of course. The ball is squarely in her court."

"What will you do with Mildred in town?"

"I'll have to be watching my back, for sure."

I made the turn into the hospital lot and helped El inside. I slapped the bell. *Ting!* When nobody came I hit it again, maybe a few too many times from the look the rotund blond gave me when she approached the counter. She sat and took El's insurance cards and driver's license, scanning them, and tapped her fingers on the keyboard with El's remaining info.

We were instructed to wait in the waiting room, but a friendly face smiled at me. "Grandma." Sophia hugged me. "What are you doing here?"

"Oh, Eleanor has nail marks on her arm. I thought it looked bad enough to warrant a trip here. I'd hate to see the poor dear bleed to death." I glanced in the waiting room. "It looks like we'll be waiting quite a while."

"Maybe not." Sophia waltzed us through a door that led into the back as protests shot from the waiting room.

As Eleanor sat on the exam table, Sophia busied herself in the corner. I hadn't seen Sophia in a while. She was athletic and ran daily on the shores of Lake Huron with her new-found buddy, Trooper Sales. Her powder-blue nurse scrubs really accentuated her deeply tanned skin. Her dark hair was swept up for work, revealing her heavily-freckled, heart-shaped face. I never knew what secrets she hid from me. Even when a dark look came across her face, she played if off like nothing was bothering her. Far be it for me to pry. She was an adult, after all.

41

Sophia smiled at Eleanor. "Let me see, Eleanor."

Eleanor held her arm tight to her body and shook her head.

"El, would you quit acting like a child!" I finally shouted.

"I saved your ass, don't forget."

Back to the past again. I frowned. "I'm sure not gonna because you'll be reminding me every chance you get."

Eleanor stuck her tongue out at me and showed Sophia her scratch.

"Doesn't look too bad, just a skin tear."

"I hate skin tears," she pouted.

Skin tears are part of every senior's life. Our skin gets so thin that the least little thing can rip it apart. Problem is that you can't get it stitched up because there simply isn't enough skin.

Sophia busied herself cleaning Eleanor's wound and wrapped it with gauze, using as little tape as possible. "There you go, good as new. I'd suggest you get some arm protectors," which she preceded to hand to Eleanor, and carefully placed on her arms.

"Ugh, I look like the Mummy!" She held her arms up, bobbling across the room toward me.

"It's not your fault, dear. You just have thin skin."

"How come you don't?"

"I sure do. Don't you remember my reactions to the gypsies comments earlier."

"You were having a meltdown."

"Thanks, Sophia." I hugged her.

"I don't suppose you were planning to tell me how you got that bruise on your cheek?"

"What!" I ran to the mirror. "Oh, that. Well ... I..."

She tapped her foot. "Just like I thought," she smiled. "You two stay out of trouble," Sophia said, her knowing stare leading me to believe that she knew she was asking the impossible.

My mouth turned down and I had to ask Sophia, "Have you heard from your mother recently?"

Sophia's face dropped and she pursed her lips tightly together. An awkward silence followed and I exchanged a soulful glance with her. "Well, then ... thanks for patching El up." I turned away and walked back into the waiting room while Eleanor used the restroom. Where is my daughter Martha and why hadn't she contacted Sophia, at least? I could fathom the idea that she was mad at me, but her own daughter... It just didn't make any sense.

CHAPTER SIX

We left the emergency room as the clouds were rolling in from Lake Huron. I sure hoped a storm wasn't coming with it. The last one had rattled my nerves something fierce and my poor cat Duchess was shaking so bad it gave me pause to worry. *Didn't animals sense impending doom?*

As we hopped back in the Caddy, I drove towards town. The streets were crowded with tourists and I had to keep my eyes peeled to the road. Tourists had the habit of jumping off the curb and crossing busy US 23 without warning.

"Can we roll by the bank? I need to make a withdrawal," El asked. "I have my eye on a new pink ensemble at Clean Sweep."

"Clean what? Huh?"

"It's a new salon that sells the most amazing apparel."

"Do they have a massage parlor in the back?" I laughed. The last time El suggested a store it sold adult products.

She waved to the bikini-clad tourists that

danced past us at the red light. "No, but you'll see soon enough."

"The anticipation is killing me."

"I'm not sure if you noticed, but kill isn't a word either of us should be using."

I raised a brow. "True, but with you there is no telling what kind of place it really is."

"Well, I don't care how you just said that, Aggie," she chuckled. "Plus, what the owners do on their free time is none of my concern."

I rolled my eyes as I turned into the bank parking lot. From the size of the crowd, it must be payday like everywhere today. "I hope they didn't misplace your money, dear. Are you sure you have—"

"They better have my money or we'll be doing a bank job."

"You shouldn't say things like that out loud," I said as we strolled through the parking lot. "That might just be grounds for arrest."

"Oh, phooey. Folks are way too sensitive these days."

"They kinda have to these days, old girl. We live in some troubled times."

Just as we entered, Eleanor was yanked to the right by a man wearing a ski mask. "Everybody on the floor or Grandma gets it!"

I froze momentarily and dropped to the floor, right next to Dorothy Alton, Eleanor's rival.

"We don't care if you kill grandma ... I mean the one you are holding there," Dorothy said. Her eyes widened when I glared at her.

"Let's just take it easy, fella. No sense in getting yourself in an uproar," I said. "Plus, plenty of us grannies in this bank." I sneered at Dorothy.

The bank robber started dancing about real nervous-like. "Get on the floor, Grandma," he said to Eleanor who dropped, rolled and laid stomach first on the floor ... her legs and arms spread out.

This is the last thing I had expected, Eleanor spread eagle at the bank. She still clutched her pink purse like it was a life-preserver.

Mr. Ski Mask hastily glanced outside and while he was turned ... Eleanor jumped to her feet, pink revolver in hand. "Freeze, sucker!"

He reacted by pointing his gun straight at Eleanor. It was the shakiest gun in Michigan as both El and the gunman stood there in a face-off of fire-power.

"Drop the gun, Granny. I don't want to shoot you!"

"You drop the gun!" El shouted.

"Seriously, I will shoot you!"

"Why don't you get a job and quit terrifying these kind folks," I said. I gulped as he turned toward me. "You're gonna get it first, Grandma." His finger squeezed the trigger and I shook,

47

made my peace with God and was ready to meet my maker until—

Eleanor swung her purse and hit the gunman squarely in the head. His gun slipped from his hand and went off with a resounding boom that luckily only hit the ceiling fan above his head.

"Boom ... pow ... ouch!" was all any of us heard as the gunman was pinned beneath the bronze ceiling fan that was quite sizable. *God love a banker with a tight budget.*

I scrambled to my feet and kicked the gun away.

El ran to me. "I didn't want to shoot him. I was afraid someone might get hurt. Besides the gunman that is."

"Good thinking."

Just then the perp jumped up and ran out of the bank. His skinny legs moved like the dickens.

"Is everyone okay?" I asked, searching the crowd.

"Would you help me up, Frank?" Dorothy Alton yelled. He, of course, kept his hearing aid turned down like always and didn't hear a thing she said but moved when she gave him a well-deserved kick.

Frank hauled himself off the floor and helped his wife up. "You know I can't hear that well!" he shouted. I had never heard Frank talk above a whisper to his wife of fifty plus years.

Dorothy began to cry. "I'm going home to mother!"

"I hope you'll both be very happy at the cemetery because that's where she lives now!"

Sirens blared and bubble lights lit up the darkening sky that looked darker than before we entered the bank. Troopers busted into the place like they were gonna save the day. Truth is, that if the perp was still here, we'd be as good as dead—not so with a Pink Lady revolver at hand.

"You can put your guns down. I know how much you cops like to shoot bad guys, but the bank robber is long gone."

Trooper Sales whirled to face me. He stared first at the ceiling and back down at the ceiling fan on the floor. "I hope this doesn't have anything to do with a Pink Lady revolver."

"Of course not!" I smiled. "I have no idea what happened. I think I might have early stages of dementia."

"How convenient."

I twisted to look at El who shrugged. "Isn't it, though?"

"I won't be finding any spent .38 cartridges, then?"

"Only from the bad guy," I said diplomatically.

"You should have seen my Eleanor stand up to that bad guy," Mr. Wilson said from a chair in the corner, his decrepit old bony body hid from view the whole time. "I was so worried, Peaches."

"Peaches, my ass. What happened to the retired school teacher, Meredith Thomas?"

"I was just trying to get you jealous, ole girl," Mr. Wilson spat.

El turned her attention back toward Trooper Sales. "Aggie and I came to the bank and this ruffian grabbed me and threatened my life, if you need to know." El bent her head and when she looked back at the trooper she was crying. "I-I was s-so scared." She bellowed for a moment. "He told me to lay spread eagle on the bank floor. It reminded me of a *Billy Jack* movie."

The troopers snickered.

My hand flew to my hips. "It's not funny. He held a gun to El's head and then he was gonna shoot me if El hadn't intervened when she did."

"How did the fan fall down if she didn't crack off a shot?" Peterson asked.

I started, "His gun discharged when El smacked him with her purse. We're all lucky to be alive."

"I'll agree with that. You should have just cooperated. He could have killed one of you," Trooper Sales cut in.

"That would look good on your resume, Sales," Sheriff Peterson said from the doorway. "Have a bunch of old folks shot during a bank robbery."

Sales glared at him. "I'm thinking that might just make your day, huh? I mean, why not blame me."

Peterson sneered. "I should get extra pay to put up with you troopers."

Thank God they were here. Sheriff Peterson is just as shady as they come and what audacity speaking to Trooper Sales like that! "If you ask me the troopers are the ones making the biggest contribution here. What took you so long? Was there a long wait at Tim Horton's donut shop?"

Peterson approached me. "Aggie, why does it not surprise me to see you here? Wherever there is a dead body or major crime, you're in the middle of it."

"We were just innocent bystanders this time around," I insisted.

"I bet." He rolled his eyes.

"Aggie is right," El said. "The bank robbery was already in progress."

"El, don't waste your breath talking to the sheriff. He won't believe a kind word about me. That is until he checks the surveillance tapes." *Bazinga!*

"I might if you kindly left town," he added.

"You're dreaming, Sheriff." I glared. "Unless you plan to pay for a trip to Florida for El and me." I grinned.

He glared at me as his face reddened, but he clammed up real quick.

I stared outside at the greenish clouds as they rolled in off the lake. "Wow, that is some storm rolling in."

The fuzz looked out the window and their radios went off. "Tornado warning. Take cover immediately."

"Everybody to the safe!" the teller, Peggy, shouted.

"Get your ass moving, Wilson," I said.

"I'm moving as fast as I can," he said as he moved his walker along.

Sheriff Peterson scooped the old man up into his arms and carried him back.

"Get your hands off of me. I don't go that way, I tell you!" Wilson stated.

We all huddled down on the floor and waited. It was hot and somebody wasn't wearing any deodorant as the smell of body odor took over.

I glared at the Sheriff. "You stink."

"It's not my fault that I perspire more than regular folks!"

I pressed my shirtsleeve against my nose as we heard a rumbling overhead. We couldn't see a thing and that made it worse, somehow. I'd survived a few storms here in Tawas, but none of them had me huddling with the state's finest and Sheriff Peterson; of course.

"No use calling in the canine unit now," Trooper Sales sputtered. "That bank robber is gonna be long gone."

I shuddered. "I just hope the town is still standing after this storm passes us by."

"Have faith," Dorothy said as she began reciting the Lord's Prayer out loud.

Ten minutes later, Sales' portable went off announcing the all clear. We all exited the safe under the watchful eye of the troopers. I guess they wanted to make sure we didn't pocket anything of value. *Geez, it's not like the cash is laid out in the open.*

The window had a gaping hole from a tree that smashed through it, and debris filled the lobby of the bank. We carefully made our way over the branches and as I saw a sandal, I picked it up. "Hey, I think I found my lost sandal." But as I tried to put it on, "Nope, it's way too small."

Sales made a call alerting more troopers to the scene to secure the bank and turned to the bank manager. "You better phone this in."

She ran toward the phone, picked it up with a trembling hand, and made her call.

Peterson fetched Mr. Wilson's walker for him, obviously not so willing to carry him back to where he snatched him up. When we left the bank, it looked quite a mess. Tree branches were scattered across the parking lot with a huge limb that had landed smack on the sheriff's car. I'm not sure if it was an act of God or maybe an act of karma.

"Jesus Christ all mighty!" Peterson bellowed. "That was a new squad car."

"Figures. I'm sure we're all gonna get a tax increase, for sure."

"Maybe they should increase the lot rent at the campground," he snapped.

I ignored him and El and I went back to her car. "If you need any more info about the bank robbery, contact me."

"Not so fast," Peterson bellowed. "Did you recognize the perp?"

"Nope."

"And the robbery was already in progress?"

"You got it."

Trooper Sales waved us off. "We'll roll back the tapes and be in touch if they don't jive with what you say."

"God dammit, Sales, is that it?" Peterson spat.

"You want those two hanging around for the rest of the investigation?" he asked, puzzled.

We jumped in the Caddy and tooled right outta there before the good sheriff made me even madder. Sure, I wondered about the bank robbery, but I was more concerned about the murder at the Butler Mansion. At least I was sure that was the case.

"Awful, that man saying that about you, Aggie. I mean, nothing wrong with living in a camper, right?"

"Nope, I just want to get back and check on Duchess. Poor dear is gonna be scared straight."

"Into what, a straightjacket?"

"I don't think they make those for cats, El. You might need one from time to time though."

"That could be fun. Just call me Fifty Shades of Granny."

"Now that is the sickest thing I have ever heard you say."

"Really? And after all this time. Come on, Aggie, I have said much worse."

"So what's the deal with Wilson?"

"Oh, nothing. He just fancies Meredith Thomas these days."

"She's a retired teacher?"

"I guess. What subject, I haven't a clue. I just had enough of old Mr. Wilson. I decided I'd be a better cougar."

"Cougar? You mean..."

"Yup. I fancy me a younger man, maybe sixty."

I laughed. I couldn't help it. "But you're eighty-two. Okay, okay, sixty would be young to you, then."

"What happened to your man? Has he called since he left town?"

I shook my head. "Nope, and I don't much care if he does. I'm not gonna wrap my life around a man no how. We have a business to run and it doesn't involve any man, that's for sure."

"What does it involve?"

"For the moment, that dead guy at the Butler Mansion."

"How we gonna dig up clues about him?"

"Simple Simon. We're gonna go to his funeral or at least do a visitation."

Eleanor chuckled. "It's a start, I suppose."

"I heard they opened a new funeral home in town, Happy Bear something."

"Happy Bear Funeral Home?" Eleanor gasped. "Why, that is the strangest name for a funeral home I ever did hear."

"That's true, but it will at least be entertaining. Imagine the owners wanted to put a smile into death."

"I bet the funeral director is smiling all the way to the bank, eh?"

"Probably. They had better hope that Mr. Butler has an insurance policy, at least."

"I almost wonder if his wife is on the policy or maybe Herman inherited more than the house."

"Good thinking, El. I knew going into business with you was the right move."

"We make one hell of a team."

I pulled into the campground and sticks were littered here, too. Luckily my Winnebago was virtually untouched.

When I went inside, Duchess jumped up in my arms, her poor body shaking. I sat and rubbed her under the chin something fierce. "It's okay girl, I'm here now," I said.

"I'll leave you two alone. I best check out my own house."

"Don't kill anyone on the way."

"I'll try not to unless I run into the bank robber."

"Like you'd know if you met him on the street. Did you forget he wore a mask?"

"I can smell a criminal a mile away."

I rolled my eyes as El left and felt a jolt as she backed into the pole that held up my awning and it crashed to the ground. "Thanks, El," I said out loud. "I sure hope she don't kill anyone for real, Duchess." She looked up at me as if interested in what I was saying. "It's not like I can tell the woman not to drive. It's like talking to a box of rocks sometimes. Okay, so all the time."

I mused about the Butler Mansion some more. *Did the widow kill him or what?* She sure acted guilty, but who knows, really. It could be the ole cloak and dagger. If this investigative stuff taught me anything, it was to find out all the facts first before passing judgment. There is always a red herring to throw you off the trail.

Did I really see more than the widow and maid or were my eyes just playing tricks on me? I should get them checked just in case. It sure couldn't hurt. I should drag El with me; it's obvious she needs it more than I do. Now I'm gonna have to get someone strong over here to help me fix my awning. It's moments like these that make me wish that I had a man around, like Andrew. It sure was comforting to have someone to hold every once in awhile. He was in town for such a brief amount of time that I just felt we didn't get time to connect other than the physical part. Not that it was bad mind you, far from it. Who knew at my age that I could do anything other than cuddle?

"Stop thinking about him, Aggie!" I yelled. Duchess picked her head up and blinked at me. I'm not sure if that was a signal to hush or quit fussing over a man that is just long gone. Another thing I missed was my house. In my opinion, they couldn't re-build it fast enough. Of course, nothing wrong with chilling at Eleanor's beach house. Maybe I should have just moved in like she had asked, but I didn't want to put her out. Who knows, it might have just worked. El and I spend so much time together that we are practically a couple, something more than a few had pointed out.

I made myself a pot of hot tea and decided the best thing I could do is just get a good night's sleep. What with a dead body, fight at the beach with my arch-enemy, and the bank robbery, it's enough to wish for easier days. *What ever happened to retirement? I'm about as far away from that as China.* Who knows what life had in store for El and me around the corner. I just knew that whatever comes our way we would face it together.

CHAPTER SEVEN

I awoke not to blinding sunlight or loud noises, but to Duchess's ass in my face. Even if she was just a cat, she could sure let out the gas. While I contemplated moving her gently and face her wrath, I decided to shove her off the bed instead. I was extra careful to make sure there was a double layer of blankets between her and me. It's always the rule to go by if you live with Duchess. Her teeth are like living on a razor's edge and I'd much prefer not to live that close to the edge. At seventy-two, I had better things to visit the doctor for.

So focused was I in thinking about Duchess that I realized that I was missing my uppers—like dentures. I hauled ass off to the bathroom, but they weren't in my denture cup either! *Where in tarnation could they be? Did I lose them on the beach when Mildred slapped me?*

Right then, Duchess was batting something around, making an awful racket. I thought at first a mouse had gotten inside, but knowing that was

59

a remote possibility I ran into the kitchen and sure enough that damn cat of mine was batting around my uppers!

"Stupid cat!" I yelled at her. She stared up at me with large cat eyes. You know, like when they are ready to attack? I thought over my options of trying to maneuver around her, but opted instead to grab a can of room deodorizer. I didn't have to even spray it. Duchess ran away like the devil was chasing her. There are two things she hates, water and spray bottles of any type.

I looked outside and remembered last night's episode of Eleanor driving badly which resulted in my awning crashing down. Now I needed to call someone up to fix the dang thing for me. I need to personally come down to the Secretary of the State: that's where we get out driver's licenses from in Michigan. I have half a mind to ask them to consider pulling Eleanor's driver's license permanently. I know that sounds harsh, but I'm only thinking about keeping the public safe.

Just then I heard quite a racket, looked out my window, and saw Chris and Curtis Hill raising my awning. I nearly had a heart attack on the spot. My friend Rosa Lee is a peach, but her boys are bad to the core. I did the only thing any self-respecting senior citizen would do. I dialed 911.

Within ten minutes, my awning was back up and the sheriff was parked next to my Mustang.

Why can't a deputy show up for a change instead of ole Peterson.

I stumbled down the steps.

"What's the 911 about, Aggie?" the sheriff asked.

"Well, these boys were messing with the awning of my Winnebago and I got scared that they were trying to..."

Curt, the larger of the two, said, "Eleanor called us and asked us to come over and fix the awning for you."

"Oh, well, I-I d-didn't know." My eyes darted between the Lee boys and the sheriff. "I'm sorry, I had no idea she called you boys."

Curt, who wore cut-off jeans and was chewing a piece of wheat between his teeth, laughed. His blond hair was buzz cut just like his brother, Chris. "My ma would cuff me real hard if I did anything to you, Miss Agnes."

Chris nodded. "Ma told us to say hello and for you to drop on by sometime."

"And where would that be?"

"The law closed down her medicinal marijuana operation. She has a quaint little shop where Roy's Bait & Tackle used to be. She got it for a real sweet deal," Chris said.

"What's she selling this time, boys?" Peterson asked with raised brow.

"Potpourri," Curt replied.

"I bet. Tell your ma I'll be around some time to check it out. Knowing your ma the way I do, there is no telling what I'll find." Peterson walked back to the squad car labeled 'Deputy'. It might be awhile before his car was fixed from the storm yesterday.

"Thanks, boys. I'm sorry I went off the deep end. Would you like a cup of coffee?"

Curt eyed my Winnebago with interest. "I think we best be moving on. You know how *some* folks like to talk."

I nodded as the boys turned tail, jumped into their truck with a Confederate flag that swung from the truck bed, and shot off like a bullet.

I let out a sigh of relief. The last thing I needed was for those boys to come into my trailer. I appreciated that El felt guilty enough to have the boys fix my awning, but really, they were quite a menace. I loved Rose Lee Hill to death, but her boys—not so much. Still, it's nice to have a little manpower. *At least now I know if I ever need a helping hand or extra guns, I could count on those boys.*

I went back inside and made breakfast. Eleanor showed up at my door not ten minutes later, dressed to the nines in lavender slacks and a cream and floral silk shirt. When I opened the door, I snickered as I looked at the tennis shoes on her feet.

"What?" she giggled. "These are the most comfortable shoes I own."

"Are we going somewhere today?"

"Happy Bear Funeral Home."

"I doubt they have Herman Butler laid out this quick."

She snickered. "Sure do. Word is the widow wants him buried real quick-like."

"Wasn't there an autopsy performed, at least? Surely there has to be one before they bury him."

"His injuries seem consistent with a fall—or so the new coroner said—so one wasn't performed."

"I suppose it would be hard to tell if he was whacked in the head before he fell unless they did an autopsy, which is standard policy with a suspicious death."

"Highly unlikely that could ever be proved now," El said. "Did you meet Jeremy yet? He's the new medical examiner. He just moved from Gratiot County just a few months past."

"Is that right, now?" I thought about it for a moment and then said, "Sounds like the new examiner has a lot to learn about procedures."

"Maybe," El grinned. "I hope he's cuter than the last one, and younger."

"Oh, El, you'll never change."

El's eyes twinkled. "Nope." She stared at the kitty-cat clock on the wall, the one with the moving eyes, and changed the subject. "Let's get over to the funeral home before we miss anything."

"It's not what you'd call a social engagement, you know."

"Who says it isn't? I wonder who is gonna be there? Seeing as how Herman was from outta town, maybe nobody will show."

"Nobody except a couple of gawking seniors, that is."

I threw on a sun-yellow dress that was about the only one I had. The rest had burned up in the fire. When I stepped back into the kitchen, Eleanor erupted into a fit of the giggles, her belly moving like the ocean was inside.

"And just what is your problem?" I asked in indignation. "It's the only dress I have."

"You look lost under all those ruffles."

She was right. This dress was all ruffles. They even blew into my face and I had to blow them away. "I don't see what else I can do unless you want to stop by Walmart."

"You look like Big Bird!" Eleanor again went into a fit of the giggles until I gave her my evil eye. "We don't have time to shop. We need to get over to the funeral home."

"Well, I sure would love to catch Betty Lou there."

"At least we can agree on something for a change," she smirked.

I proceeded outside with Eleanor and spotted my neighbor across the way—Leotyne, who went to pointing and laughing, jumping up and down like the complete nut job that I had already pegged her to be. Seriously, what had I done to deserve this kind of neighbor? I promised tomorrow I'd file some kind of complaint. I mean, isn't putting a curse on someone against some kind of camping ground ordinance?

We barreled up the road and arrived at Happy Bear Funeral Home, which was kind of easy to spot as it was covered with pink and yellow streamers and balloons.

There were times in your life where you'd have the occasional funeral to attend, but at my age it's commonplace.

"Happy Bear Funeral Home seems like a strange name for a funeral home to me," Eleanor remarked.

"Somehow happy and funeral just don't go together."

"Unless you're the mortician."

"I bet he's happy all the time."

"And most likely laughing all the way to the bank."

We parked, and as we made our way inside, a young woman dressed in a red dress with a white ruffled apron greeted us.

"Welcome to Happy Bear Funeral Home, where death is never a reason to be sad." Her plastic smile was worthy of a late night infomercial for zit cream. She obviously took her time learning the lines. The least I could do is play along.

I smiled. "Really? Is your mother laid out here?"

"W-Why, no," the girl said. "It's a motto the owner came up with. Isn't it great?"

"Very clever," I replied. "In a morbid kinda way."

"Would you care for any refreshments?"

That got Eleanor's attention. "What kind of snacks do you have?"

She presented a silver platter filled with, what else, but finger sandwiches.

Eleanor gasped. "I sure hope they aren't made from real fingers."

"Of course not!" the girl laughed.

As we made our way toward the viewing room, I couldn't help but overhear the voices that carried from inside an office.

"I told you, I want Herman cremated," a woman's voice said.

I recognized Betty Lou standing just inside the office.

"I explained this to you already, Mrs. Butler. There are very specific instructions in how the remains are to be handled. All Butler descendants must be buried in the Butler family cemetery on the hill."

"I know, I know all about that quaint little

resting place, but I don't even plan to stay so why plant him there?"

"So you don't plan to stay in the Tawas area?"

"No, we just came here because Herman inherited that huge house and all. I plan to put it on the auction block first chance I get."

"Why such a rush?" The funeral director cleared his throat. "The will hasn't even been read yet."

"Herman didn't have a will, and as his wife and sole heir, I stand to inherit everything."

"Well, then, that's none of my concern. The funeral is taken care of by the Butler Foundation."

"The what?"

"It's a charitable foundation that funds activities in the area. Why, just last year it helped pay for a new wing at the County Medical Center. It also earmarked funds for the funeral costs of the Butlers' funerals."

"That is a load of baloney. So you're saying this Butler Foundation paid for a new wing at a nursing home?"

"Yes, that's right. It's one of the main contributors."

"Well, I'll be retaining a lawyer and looking into the matter. I'm selling that mansion, Mr. Henderson, and moving the hell out of here."

I tried to move, but my knee didn't cooperate and I froze just as Betty Lou nearly ran into me.

She was dressed in yet another strumpet dress, although this one was black.

"You!" she shouted. "Why are you here?"

"I came to show my respects."

"Somebody needs to show you out the damn door." Betty Lou locked eyes with both El and me. "Somebody get these women out of here."

The funeral director rushed from his office, his rosy cheeks flushed to a point that they looked painted on. "Now, now, what is the problem, Mrs. Butler? These ladies are upstanding members of the community, and as such, are welcome to be here."

Betty Lou huffed. "Fine, let the old hags stay then. I'm leaving and will be back later." She rushed outside like the place was on fire.

"I-I'm sorry. You're Agnes Barton and Eleanor Mason, right?"

"Why, yes, we are." Eleanor said. "And who would you be?"

"I'm Martin Henderson, owner of Happy Bear Funeral Home." Martin ran a hand over his sparse white hair before offering it to the ladies; his paunch barely noticeable under the cut of his fine tailored suit.

"Why, aren't you a handsome devil," El's eyes searched the room. "Is your wife around?"

"Oh, no, my wife died a few years back. Massive heart attack."

El batted her eyelashes. "Oh, my. I'm so sorry, Mr. Henderson."

"Don't be silly." He smiled. "Death is another journey is all."

"That sounds awful," I spat. "It's like you're happy about her death."

"Yes, I am, Agnes." He held up his hand. "Don't get me wrong here, but before my wife died she laid out a very detailed plan on how she wanted her funeral to be."

"She wanted you to be happy?" I motioned around me at the balloons and streamers. I couldn't help but sneer when I said it.

"She wanted it to be like a party, and that is basically the concept behind Happy Bear Funeral Home."

"This place is gonna go under real fast."

"Oh, Aggie. Don't give him a hard time. I love the idea," Eleanor smiled. "I'm single and available, Mr. Henderson."

He laughed slyly. "Please, call me Martin, Miss Eleanor."

"Seriously, can we view the body if you two are done?" I walked in the large room that had rather sinister looking paintings hanging on the wall. "This doesn't look too happy to me."

"Those are the paintings of the Butler family. I must admit they are quite serious looking, but men in those days were quite serious about business," Mr. Henderson said.

"Where did they make all their money?"

"They were in the shipping and logging business, the best I can recollect," El replied.

Mr. Henderson cleared his throat. "Old money, from the sounds of it."

"Quite," El said as she gave the funeral director a hard stare. "I have lived in the area for twenty years whereas my friend Agnes is newer to the area."

"I see. Well ... I have only recently moved here from Grayling, Michigan. My father owned a funeral parlor there and I took it over when he died fifteen years ago. With my wife gone, I decided to sell the business and relocate to the East Tawas area."

"Why is that?" I asked.

"I have always loved the Tawas area and wanted to move here and live on Lake Huron."

"You have lake front property?" El asked. "I live on the lake too, but it's not much bigger than a cabin really."

"Nothing wrong with that, dear. I kind of get lonely living all alone in a large house." He flirted with Eleanor who was just sucking it up!

I changed the subject "So what did you think of Mr. Butler's body?"

"I'm not sure what you mean?"

"Did he look like he might have just fallen out of a window."

"Well, I'm not sure about that one. I'm no coroner."

"No, but I'm sure you have seen bodies that had similar injuries to them."

"Well, this is a rather odd question, Agnes, and I feel a little uneasy about answering it."

El gave me a kick. "Leave that man alone, Aggie."

Martin swallowed and led us away from the pack of spectators.

I pursed my lips. "I'm sorry, but we heard that an autopsy wasn't done. Is that right?"

"I'd love to help you. It's just that, well ... I can't."

"And why is that?" I snapped.

"It would be against my policy. Maybe you should ask Mr. Butler's widow."

"I told you so, Aggie," El shrugged.

"Oh, you did not! Fine, it's just that I'm really surprised that the sheriff didn't insist on one."

"Isn't it standard procedure, Aggie?" Eleanor asked.

"I'm not really sure, but I'd love to find out."

I thanked Martin, and El and I approached the body. The bald-headed body that laid in the casket did look like the same man we had seen yesterday, except for the make-up, mind you.

"Why do they layer the make-up so thick?" El frowned. "It's just creepy."

"I suppose to make them look alive."

"Well, it's not working."

I stared across the room and saw Andrew Hart speaking to a woman with silver hair.

Why, that rat! Andrew is back in town with a mystery woman in tow? I could tell by the way she clasped Andrew's shirt cuff that they were more than just acquaintances, much more. At this point, he didn't notice either El or me, so intent was he on the woman next to him. *Is she his new girlfriend?* She's tall and thin as a stalk of corn in fall. Her silver hair was styled and spiked to perfection like she was from New York City ... *I bet not a strand of hair would blow out of place in a hurricane. They can both go to Hades for all I care.* I dragged a startled Eleanor off before she had time to react.

We made our way back to El's Caddy. "Did you see that woman with Andrew?" El asked. "You didn't tell me he was back in town."

"I didn't know!" I said as we climbed into the Caddy, spun onto the road, and raced to the sheriff's department.

"Did you two break up?"

"We had an argument before he left and he promised he'd come back. I guess he just didn't mention with whom."

"Oh, my. Do you want me to get rid of her?" she giggled. "We could give her some Cat Lady's moonshine. It about killed you the one time you drank it," she laughed. "We'll need a boat and chains and weights though." She sucked one finger into her mouth.

My eyes widened. "What in the world for?"

"To get rid of the body, silly."

"If I didn't know you were joking I'd turn you into the state police."

El rolled her eyes. "I'm kinda a joking and kinda not. Is that a bad thing?"

"Yes! We solve crimes, we don't perpetrate them," I snapped.

CHAPTER EiGHT

When I made the turn into the parking lot of the sheriff's department, the lot was packed. We had to park quite a distance from the building, as even all the handicapped spaces were taken.

As El and I huffed and puffed our way up the path, we saw a man hop into his car that was parked in the space that should be reserved for the handicapped.

"Oh, look, Aggie. He's handicapped."

"Yup, he can't read," I added.

Eleanor took a stance behind his car, legs spread and hands on hips, right behind the car in question.

"El, please, move before you get run over."

"Not until I give this jerk a piece of my mind."

I rolled my eyes. I knew this was gonna be a scene I'd rather not witness.

The car inched back, but Eleanor, with a menacing look in her eye, glared at the car like she was sizing up an opponent.

The occupant of the car moved his arm out of the window and motioned Eleanor with a wave of his hand. She didn't budge one inch. Then he gave her the finger and she reached into her bag and pulled her Pink Lady revolver out.

"Eleanor, put that thing away before somebody gets hurt."

"Oh, somebody will. Him."

The car door flew open and the young man started screaming. "She's pointing a gun at me! Somebody help!"

El put her gun away. "Big baby, it's not even loaded."

"You don't look handicapped to me," I added.

"You old bats better get out of my way or else I'm telling Uncle Clem."

I stared at this young skinny fella. The tee he wore was about as tight as the skinny jeans he wore. I scratched my head for a moment. "Clem Peterson is your uncle?"

"Like in Sheriff Peterson?" Eleanor laughed.

"Y-Yes. Wh-why?"

"Don't you know handicapped spots are for handicapped people?" Eleanor shouted. "We had to park a half mile down the street. Don't you know us older folks have medical issues and bad constitutions?" El began to fan herself and slumped to the ground.

"Oh great, see what you did now? The poor dear has fallen out. If she dies it'll be your fault and I'll testify at your murder trial," I insisted.

"I didn't kill her!" he cried. "I park here all the time and nobody ever says squat."

I knelt to check El's pulse and played like I was giving her CPR until the man ran inside the sheriff's department. "Stop it now, El. He's running for reinforcements."

I helped her up and she was in a fit of the giggles, but tried to look serious when the sheriff ran outside with a defibrillator.

"What in the hell is going on?" Peterson yelled.

"Your nephew there was parked in the handicapped spot and El and him got into a little discussion about it is all." I took in a hard breath. "We had to park clear to the street." I waved my handicapped parking permit in his face.

"She was just on the ground while that other one told me I was gonna be charged with murder."

Peterson turned to his nephew. "I told you a thousand times not to park in the handicapped spot, Clint."

"Are you gonna give him a ticket or let him off the hook 'cause he's related to you?" Eleanor taunted Peterson.

"Like I have time for this crap." Peterson stomped his way inside, returned a few minutes later with a ticket in hand, and gave it to Clint.

"You have to be kidding, Uncle. Tell me you're not giving your own nephew a ticket."

"It's a sizable fine so you best find a job here in town to pay me back while you're here."

"But it's summer vacation," he whined.

"Sorry, kid," Peterson said and walked back inside.

El, always one to get in the last dig, stuck her tongue out at Clint. "I guess we won't be seeing you at the beach."

I pushed Eleanor inside where the sheriff awaited us. "In my office," he said. "Somehow I figured you two would show up."

We followed the sheriff and felt every eye in the room on us. When we stepped into the sheriff's office, he closed the door behind us.

He sat and rocked back on his leather chair waiting for us to speak, but I was eyeing up his office. He had a computer on his desk with a few picture frames scattered about. Along one wall were three file cabinets. It was quite a tiny room really. A large window displayed the view of Lake Huron.

"Nice office," I finally said.

"Thanks," he choked out. "Is there a purpose for your visit today or should I wait to find out on the six o'clock news?"

"I was just at Happy Bear Funeral Home. I overheard there wasn't an autopsy performed on Herman Butler."

"Happened to overhear via a glass held to a door, perhaps," he mocked.

"Heck no," El confessed. "I'd rather not divulge our source, but it's common knowledge around town."

"You mean gossip, but just to get the two of you out of my office, I'll confirm that the coroner didn't feel an autopsy was warranted in this case."

"Doesn't one have to be performed? I mean, surely you can't rule out foul play."

"Of course not, Agnes. We are still investigating and keeping a watchful eye on the widow, but really there is just not enough evidence to suggest a crime was committed."

I gave Peterson the eye. "I watch CSI every week and an autopsy is always performed."

"And falls are fairly frequent for the older population."

"Not from a third story window, Sheriff," I countered.

"The decision has already been made, so drop it. If we ordered autopsies every time one of you seniors died, we'd be doing them all the time."

"Something I need to know about, Sheriff. Like is there an unusual amount of senior citizens dying of late?"

He opened his mouth but then clammed up.

"Her blaming a ghost wasn't enough for you, huh? I don't know why I keep trying to talk to you when you're so dead set on disagreeing with me on every account."

He rolled forward, the wheels of his chair straining under his weight. "Then find something to convince me it was not an accident."

"When I find out I'm right about Herman's death, you'll eat your words."

"You do that and I'll send the two of you on a trip to Florida."

We left, and the sound of his laughter followed us to the front door.

"Did the sheriff really encourage us to investigate?" El asked.

"Sounds like it. But then again, there isn't sound proof Herman didn't fall to his death. He also knows we will investigate like always."

"True, but did he really mean it or is he setting us up? I'd hate to be arrested again."

"Really? You looked so good in cuffs." I nudged her in the ribs. "Peterson has a valid point though. We seniors are accident prone."

El snickered. "Remind me to stay clear of open windows."

Waves crashed in the distance and the aroma of fish was thick in the air. The wind had died down a bit and my thoughts trailed off. I hoped Peterson would allow us the room we needed to investigate. With law enforcement on tight budgets these days, he could sure use two extra pairs of eyes.

CHAPTER NINE

El and I sat in the Caddy parked in the one place I thought I'd never be, Clean Sweep in Tadium, Michigan. It's a quaint new spa of some sort or so Eleanor had said. Looking at the small purple building with a peacock painted near the front door, I had guessed this was gonna be a one of a kind experience.

"So why didn't they open this place in Tawas?" I asked curiously.

El grinned. "It's against some sort of ordinance."

"Really? Which one?"

"I don't know, Aggie. Quit being a sour puss and come inside with me. It's too hot to stay outside in the car."

I followed Eleanor inside where a register was located along one side with shelves built into the wall with an assortment of nail and skin care products on display. Through a pair of glass doors were racks of brightly-colored apparel and hats.

A woman stood at the ready with a tray of assorted nail polishes displayed on it. "Would you like a manicure?" the petite blond asked.

"No, we'd like to be strip mined today," El stated as she rubbed her chin.

"Oh, my!" The girl's tray rattled something fierce. "I didn't know women ... I mean, oh my, I don't know what I mean."

"You was gonna say old, right?" I laughed. I put a hand up and whispered, "Not the way to go with this one." I pointed at Eleanor.

"Right! Even us older gals like to trim the hedges every once in a while." El nudged me. "Isn't that right, Aggie?"

"I'm not certain what you're even referring to. I'm sure I don't care to know, either."

Just then, a door popped open and a young woman staggered out, her hand clasped over her lower region. I didn't have to guess any longer what kind of place this was. It was no place I cared to be, I'm quite certain.

"You can quit gawking, Aggie. Flies might be drawn in, dear," El said with a smile. "You're making that young lady at the register nervous."

"She looks like she's in distress!"

"That's how it always feels afterward. It's a perfectly normal reaction."

"Can we leave now, please?"

I had covered my womanly parts at this point.

I think I was having sympathy pains for the poor thing that wobbled out of the shop with a pained and contorted expression on her face.

The woman manning the register acknowledged El. "Hello, Eleanor. I had expected you earlier this week."

"We got tied up on a case and were too busy. This here is Agnes Barton." El thumbed toward me.

Her mouth sprung open. "Really, the famous private investigator?"

"Well, next to me, yes." Eleanor searched about the room. "Do you have time for a quick appointment or should we come back?"

"Of course I have time for two such famous investigators. Follow me into the back." She giggled. "Name's Stacey," she said over her shoulder.

Stacey was a plus-sized woman with a plus-sized personality, complete with a lopsided grin plastered on her face. Her cheeks were stained with rouge and she wore way too much blue eye shadow for a proprietor of such a business as this...or maybe not, now that I think about it.

In the back room was a lounging chair that looked like something you'd see in a dentist's office, not a place of this sort.

Stacey dusted off the seat and put a paper sheet down. "Who's first?"

"For what, exactly?" I eyed wax containers with brushes crammed into them. It didn't look a bit sanitary to me.

"We specialize in bikini waxes; of course," Stacey said, "but I imagine you two might prefer to have your facial hair done.

"I don't," I said. "If I start doing that it will grow back like a forest."

Eleanor scoffed. "Quit being a fuddy duddy. Stacey here has strip-mined the women of Tadium for the last ten months."

I shook my head. "I think not." From the expression on Stacey's face, I think she likes her job a little too much.

"I think, yes," El said as she pushed me down on the reclining chair.

I waved her off. "No thanks, dear, but I insist on clean brushes for El." I shot off the chair like it was on fire.

"Sure thing," Stacey said as she went off and returned with the items I had requested. When she returned, she said, "I heard there was an accident at the Butler Mansion."

"Really, Stacey?" I smiled as El sat down.

"Herman Butler's wife was in here before her husband died. She was going on and on about her wedding and how happy she was that she wouldn't have to struggle for money anymore."

My brow rose. "That's interesting."

"Doesn't sound like she'd want him dead then, does it, Aggie?" El added, "Seems like she might have found her golden ticket."

"That's why she makes a perfect suspect." I watched nervously as Stacey applied wax to El's hairy chin. The strips went down and were yanked off without one scream from El. "Hey, what gives?"

"I applied the Wax and Relax No Scream Cream before I came here," El said. "It does work wonders." She grinned. "Aggie, I told you she's a professional."

Out of the blue, Stacy asked, "So you suspect the widow?"

"Her husband died a little too soon after the wedding for me. Out a window no less."

"Wow, that is bad luck."

"And hardly an accident," Eleanor added.

I peered at El's face to assure her skin was intact. "Amazing."

Aggie, you should really consider getting your facial hair waxed. I hate to tell you this, but yours is getting very noticeable," she said, staring intently at my upper lip.

"That's the cruelest thing you have ever said to me, El."

"How can that be? I'm fairly certain I have said way worse things to you before," she coughed.

Eleanor cleaned up and we waltzed to the register.

"You know, Miss Agnes ... Betty Lou Butler goes to Hidden Cove every Wednesday," she frowned. "But so does Sheriff Peterson."

I sighed. "Tonight, drat. I was hoping to do some investigating, but Peterson will just get in the way."

"I could help you," Stacey grinned. "I know how to keep a man busy." She batted her eyelashes.

I choked. "Seriously?"

Eleanor patted Stacey on the back. "I think he's married, though."

Stacey grinned at that. "I know he is, but all I had planned to do was distract him. I'll keep him plenty busy," Stacey reassured me.

"So you'll help us out?" I asked, enthused.

"Sure, it'll be the closest I ever get to being an actual investigator."

We left and Eleanor lit into me. "What did you do that for? I think two investigators is enough."

"She seems real nice and we could use someone to distract the good sheriff while we do some digging. Plus, I heard they were ship-spotting there tonight."

Eleanor rubber her hands together. "Oh, I had forgotten about that. I heard it might be foggy tonight, too. It's perfect ghost-ship-spotting weather."

"See, we can kill two birds with a bat. Stacey

can get a chance to keep Peterson busy and we can hopefully spot a ghost ship."

"Hey, since when are you interested in ghost ships?"

"I haven't thought of anything else since you brought it up," I lied, but could tell by El's facial expression she wasn't buying into it.

"Who are you planning to question at Hidden Cove?"

"I was hoping we could do a little eavesdropping and play it by ear."

"You're an evil woman, Agnes. I love it, but didn't Peterson give us the go ahead to investigate?"

"Since Peterson is so intent on thinking her husband's death was an accident, you know he won't let us *really* investigate the woman without him being close by."

"He knows us too well by now, I suppose," Eleanor added. "It wouldn't surprise me if he had us watched."

"I'm quite sure he hasn't either the gumption or resources to do that."

"That's another good reason to have some senior snoops like us."

"You're right, El. We're actually doing him a favor," I winked.

CHAPTER TEN

El, Stacey, and I were in strategic positions on the deck at Hidden Cove, a little bar and grill. We were next to the railing that overlooked Lake Huron. El and I were dressed in dark clothing with Detroit Tiger ball caps on our heads. I figured when it got dark, we'd be invisible to most any passerby as the lighting on this deck at night was less than desirable. I don't think anybody would ever guess who we were. I snickered, not that it mattered. Trying to remain incognito in a small town was like trying to say the sky isn't blue. Stacey, on the other hand, wore a white ensemble with plunging neckline. Of course, her bosom was quite a bit more south, but the men who passed by didn't seem to mind.

El pointed across the room. "Look, Agnes, Betty Lou is here," El said. We spied her lingering by the doorway.

I frowned. "So is Peterson."

Stacey jumped up. "That's my cue."

I frowned. "I wonder why Peterson shows up here every Wednesday?"

Eleanor shrugged. "Beats me, but maybe he really is keeping an eye on the widow like he said."

"You should know by now I'm not counting all my chickens over that one. We can find out way more than he can."

"How right you are, Aggie. The law has its restrictions."

"That's why being an investigator is more interesting."

Stacey was laughing at whatever Peterson had said. He must have been feeling mighty uncomfortable as he yanked at his shirt.

I laughed. "He's way out of his comfort zone."

Eleanor sipped her tiny drink that had a tiny umbrella inside. "Yup. She's blocking his view, too."

A crowd filtered on the deck with drinks in hand. Since Michigan banned smoking in bars and restaurants, it was much easier to breathe out here, too. Hidden Cove didn't allow smoking on the deck, either. "Fancy meeting you here," a voice suddenly said into my ear, and I nearly jumped out of my chair.

"What in the hell?" I stared right into Andrew's eyes.

He eyed my apparel. "Cute hat and attire," he grinned.

"I think the Tigers might make it to the World Series this year."

"Since when are you into baseball?"

I cleared my throat. "Actually I don't mind watching a game."

"It's the only time she has a nap," El cut in.

I gave El the eye, but ignored her taunt and tried my best to act nonchalant. "What are you doing here?"

"Same thing as you, I expect." He stared across the lake and then in Betty Lou's direction.

I searched the room a moment before spotting the woman I had seen Andrew talking to at the funeral home.

"Maybe you should get back to your girlfriend."

His eyes narrowed. "Maybe I should."

He trounced away in a huff. I stared at his ass the whole way, too. "It's just criminal for a man to look that good at seventy," I muttered. Tears threatened to spill, but I wouldn't allow them to. "See! He's with that woman!"

"He never said that, Aggie. You just assumed it."

I sipped my wine. "He didn't dispute the fact."

"He didn't say anything about her. You did."

I grumbled under my breath. "This is the main reason I haven't bothered with men all these years."

"You are so over-blowing the situation. No committed man looks at a woman like he was looking at you, and that's all I'm saying on the subject." She shifted her gaze to the lake.

"Shhh," I said.

Betty Lou Butler walked from the doorway just then, her arm looped around a rather tall man, while another joined them.

The threesome sat the next table over from us. So as not to be noticed, I snapped my attention and watched the sun disappear from the horizon with a display of pink and orange.

"Pink sky night, sailor's delight," I said.

"What does that mean, Aggie?"

"It means it's going to be a good day tomorrow, but if pink sky day, sailors be warned."

"Is there any truth to that poem?"

"The other day it was pink at sunrise and look what kind of storm occurred. You, more than anyone else, should know it's true. You have lived on Lake Huron long enough to know first-hand."

El groaned. "You're expecting too much from my old mind."

I sat upright, shocked. "Since when did you start referring to yourself as old anything?"

Eleanor smirked. "I know, them be some fighting words."

We both hushed up and listened to the waves breaking to beach, a soothing sound that made me wish I was tucked in bed, not here.

The conversation from Betty Lou's table drifted to us. I smiled. *Things are going according to plan so far.*

"So they spotted a real ghost ship on Lake Huron," a man's voice asked.

The other man responded. "I told you so, Troy."

"I'm asking the lady here, not you, Nate."

"Yup, so they say. *Erie Board of Trade*," Betty Lou informed them.

"That is just an old ghost story, they say," Troy countered.

"If you believe that, then why are you boys even in Tawas?" Betty Lou mused.

Troy leaned in. "It sure would be an interesting show for us, although we are more into investigating haunted houses."

"I might be able to help you two out with that. It seems a ghost had pushed my husband to his death at my house. If you two could prove the house is haunted, then maybe I could clear up some loose ends and be able to sell that house."

"A ghost killed your husband?" Nate asked.

"Yes, he plunged to his death from a third floor window."

"We'd love to investigate your house. Where is it located?" Troy asked.

"It's the Butler Mansion, but I'm afraid I have been locked out," she pouted.

"Why is that?" Nate asked. "They don't believe it's really an accident or the work of a ghost?"

"No, it seems public opinion has swayed the town against me via a couple of snoopy old bats playing investigator. I had three people stop me while I was shopping at Walmart to ask me 'if I really killed my husband like Agnes Barton said'."

Eleanor started to stand, but I grabbed her arms to force her to sit. "Ouch, that hurt," she whispered.

"I know. That was the point. You know dang well we need to keep on the down low."

El adjusted her sunglasses. "I'm curious about why she was locked out."

"Very curious. Maybe the sheriff really is watching the widow, like you said." I yawned. "We need to find out who ordered the lock down."

Waves suddenly crashed to the beach at a harder pace. We jumped to our feet and all stared out into Lake Huron. In the far distance, we saw a steamship with smoke billowing behind it causing quite a smoke cloud in its wake.

"It's the *Erie*!" a woman screamed.

Soon after, the deck was overloaded with spectators and we were pushed to the rails. We splayed our arms out, grasped the railing, and tried to keep our footing.

"Watch out! Old ladies here, folks," I said.

Obviously nobody had heard us as the crowd continued to push forward like they were at a rock concert. A spotlight split the night air and flashbulbs went off in unison.

El and I just struggled to keep from being crushed beneath the weight of the crowd.

As the spotlight swept across the now dark lake, a bell sounded in the distance, but nothing was notably visible. Yet waves continued to pound the beach.

Even *I*, the unbeliever of the bunch, began to believe there really was a ghost ship. This is just impossible, because ghost ships just don't exist. I had lived near Tawas long enough, and I knew steamships don't sail the Great Lakes anymore. But, I could still smell the smoke that had billowed in the air as it drifted to where we stood gawking.

Within five minutes, the crowd dispersed and El and I could relax from the near panic we had felt. *Okay, so maybe a ghost ship could be sailing Lake Huron, but why now and not before?* It just seemed wrong, if I hadn't seen it with my own two eyes — not that I could visualize much of anything.

"The waves were certainly coming in fast," I told Eleanor. "I'm sorry for being an unbeliever."

"Did you smell the smoke, Aggie?"

"I must admit I did. I think the whole town did."

"Who would have thunk it — a real ghost ship right here in Tawas."

"Not me, that's for sure." I paused. "But you know how my mind works overtime, I just wonder if this could be a farce. How many sightings have there been lately?"

"Well, since you were *busy*, the ship has been sighted five times."

"Well, now that there's a pair of ghost hunters in town, this might just prove to be an exciting summer."

I read the initials on the back of the ghost hunter's black shirts, G.A.S.P. I started laughing out loud.

"What's so dang funny, Aggie?"

"Did you read the initials on the back of their shirts, G.A.S.P. Gasp."

El craned her neck and smirked. "I wonder what it stands for?"

I motioned to one of the ghost hunters and he came over. "I'm sorry, but can you tell me what G.A.S.P. means?"

"Certainly." He cleared his throat at our all black apparel. "Ghost Association Special Police."

I laughed out loud at that. "You do know it spells gasp, right?"

"Certainly, ma'am." He leaned in. "Are you a couple of cat burglars?"

"Nope," El said. "I haven't stolen a cat yet."

"Something wrong with how we're dressed, young man?" I asked with a serious voice.

"N-No o-of course not. It's just that you're all dressed in dark clothing and sitting practically in the dark."

"Good. Now I won't have to tell you that your hair looks like it has grown wings." It was true though, the sides of his black hair stuck out.

He patted his head. "It's supposed to look that way."

"Really? Exactly just what kind of hairdo is that?"

"It doesn't really have a name."

"I'd call it a mess," El snickered. "Would you like to borrow my brush?"

"Excuse my friend," I changed the subject. "Do you have a card? I mean in case we run into a ghost."

He handed me a card with the words G.A.S.P. and a picture of a ghost. *How unoriginal.*

My eyes widened. "Do you currently have an APB out for any ghosts in particular or just one?"

He stared in silence.

El shook her head. "Ghost police, indeed."

"Seriously, will there also be a photo of the ghosts on the most wanted board at the post office."

"Good one, Aggie. Call 1-800-Gasp if you see this orb."

"Very funny, even for a couple of old broads."

Eleanor rummaged in her purse.

I shook my head. "Oh great. She's going for her gun."

The young ghost hunter darted away. In his haste he tripped on a chair, and landed on top of a table full of drinks. As he slid to the floor, a group of girls began to beat him about the head with their purses. "Look what you did to my dress?" one shouted. "You clumsy fool!"

The crowd backed away from El and me. "I was only looking for a tissue!" El declared.

I shrugged. "False alarm. Sorry, folks," I reassured the crowd.

Sheriff Peterson strode toward us with Stacey chasing after him. "Sorry, Agnes," she said.

Peterson gave her a hard stare. "Friend of yours?" He gestured in Stacey's direction. "Could you call her off, please," he said between gritted teeth.

"Depends," El twiddled her fingers. "You plannin' to harass us?"

"Not if you call off your friend. You know I'm married. If my wife hears about this one I'm in deep shit."

I smiled. "I'd hate to be causing you any grief, Peterson. I'm just trying to do my job, same as you."

"Oh, who hired you?"

El raised her index finger in the air. "See, that's the thing. We were never actually hired by anyone."

"We did receive a phone call from a concerned citizen who informed us about Herman falling to his death." I smiled. It shouldn't be a mystery why I was investigating a murder in my own town. It should be expected.

"Concerned citizens should be calling the police, not you two."

"So, who locked the place up?" I asked. "I mean, I couldn't help but hear that the Butler Mansion was locked up."

"Happened to hear?" He snorted. "That's rich. Please tell me how two old coots like you can hear so dang well? Why can't you have hearing issues like the rest of the old folks?"

Eleanor, with one hand on her hip, took to tapping her foot. "Oh, but she does have hearing problems, she hears what she wants."

"I what?"

"Tell me something I didn't know." He yawned. "I can't tell you who might have locked up the Butler Mansion, but there is a court hearing about it tomorrow."

"Thanks, Sheriff."

He nodded and seemed a little too cocky, but whatever the case was, at least he shared some info with us. He strode away and I stopped Stacey from following.

"Aww, I was just starting to enjoy myself," Stacey frowned.

"He's a married man, didn't you just hear?" El huffed. "But Trooper Sales on the other hand is quite available."

I frowned when I noticed Sales across the room with a slim brunette. *My granddaughter!* "Why, that snake in the grass!"

El stopped me from racing right over there. "Aggie, calm down. I'm sure it's nothing."

I jerked my arm away and approached the couple. Sales eyes widened as did Sophia's.

She laughed nervously. "Gramms." She held a beer bottle tightly in her right hand.

I stared at her startled expression. "Fancy meeting you here."

She rubbed the back of her neck. "Yes, we just came from a run on the beach."

They both wore sweaty tees, shorts, and sneakers. "Since when do you drink beer?"

From between gritted teeth, "Gramms, you're embarrassing me."

"Aggie, let's leave the kids alone. I'm tired," El whined.

"She's a kid, he's far from one," I muttered as I walked through the bar and outside. When we made the turn toward El's place, I said, "I can't believe *they* were there, together."

"Aggie, she's over twenty-five, let it go. Plus, after all she's been through."

I glared at her, tears running down my face. "I'm not talking about *that*, ever you hear."

"I'm not asking you to, dear, but she needs a friend and at least Sales is an honorable man. He's not gonna cut out of line."

"And what if he does?" I sniffled.

"I'm sure Sophia can handle herself. You need to cut the apron strings."

"It would be so much easier if only my daughter Martha was here."

El frowned. "Where is she, anyhow? I mean ever since that whole business with Sophia, she hasn't been in contact with you."

"I tried numerous times to contact her, but it's like she just doesn't want anything to do with me. If Sophia has been in contact with her, it's beyond me. She didn't answer when I asked her at the hospital."

"True, Aggie, but I wonder if she just can't bring herself to talk about it."

"Oh, I don't know. When Martha was a child we were so close and now I don't even know where my baby is," I cried.

"So you're saying the great investigator hasn't figured out how to find her missing daughter?"

"She's not missing, she just chooses to stay away. I'm not sure if she even knows that Sophia is safe and sound." *How could Martha have stayed away from her own daughter?* I could deal with my own pain. Well, sort of.

I made the turn into the driveway, followed El into her house, and passed out on her lumpy couch with one thought in my mind. *I'm gonna kill Sales if he lays one hand on my granddaughter!*

CHAPTER ELEVEN

When I woke up, Eleanor was in the kitchen singing to Hank Williams, coffee mug in one hand and tongs in the other as she made breakfast. I enjoyed the fragrance of bacon and eggs as it lingered in the air. I made my way into the bathroom and when I came out, El had a cup of coffee poured into my favorite Hello Kitty mug.

I poured in vanilla creamer and swung my hips a little at the music.

"I know you're not dancing to Hank Williams. You hate him, Aggie."

"Sure do, but I need to get my body moving after sleeping on your lumpy couch all night."

Thump.

"What is that?" I asked as I walked to the patio door. The sky was grey with a few rays of sunlight peeking out, and the lake was calm.

El sipped her coffee, "That's Rattail."

There was a squirrel scratching at the door. "Seriously, didn't squirrels get you into enough trouble last year?"

"He's a good squirrel and my pet."

She opened the door and I stared when the little bugger ran into the house and climbed on the counter. El pulled a dish from the cupboard and filled it with peanuts.

"You're crazy. You can't let a squirrel in the house."

"Why not? I've had far worse in this house before, like Mr. Wilson." Her eyes twinkled.

"So you two really called it quits?"

"We were never a couple, Aggie. More of an arrangement, really. He could make one hell of a tuna casserole."

"And now he's making it for the retired school teacher."

"Just like your Andrew is doing whatever with that woman that we don't know if he is or isn't married to."

Ouch. "Things change."

El laughed at that. "I wouldn't give up on that man just yet, old girl. He still has eyes for you."

I sipped my coffee. "Maybe." I told myself to quit thinking about him, but so far no go. "He's up to something, though. He almost seemed as concerned about Betty Lou as we are. I wonder why?"

"It might be worth checking out," El pointed out as she moved to wash the dishes in the sink.

I took a shower and changed into sweats that

I had left at El's in case I spent the night here, or drank too much to drive home.

When El had changed into a green crop pants and matching tee with a dragonfly in sequins, we left for my Winnebago.

When I arrived home, Duchess attacked me on sight, and I made coffee out of habit. "Poor baby missed Mommy?" She dove out the door as Eleanor walked in. "Eleanor, you let her out."

"She let her own self out, slipped right through the door." She stared at Duchess's empty dish. "She might have to catch her own dinner. It looks like her food is all gone."

I frowned and ran out the door in search of Duchess just as a paneled station wagon drove in.

"Oh, my," Eleanor said. "Were you expecting company?"

"Maybe they are in the wrong place." I shifted my eyes over to the gypsy's campsite, but not a soul was there.

"Hi, Mom," a woman said as she walked toward me.

"Oh, my." I slumped to the ground.

"Oh, no!" Are you okay, Aggie?" El asked.

I nodded, too shocked for words. *Of all the dumb coincidences...* "Martha?" My mouth hung open, not just at her being here, but at her attire.

She wore a skin-tight jungle print ensemble that looked like it was stripped from the seventies, just like her station wagon. Her hair was pulled up into a high ponytail and red sunglasses covered her eyes.

Eleanor belly laughed. "I could almost guess you were Agnes' daughter. I bet you shop at the same stores."

"Where have you been?" I asked. "I have tried calling you. Does Sophia know you're here?" Tears filled my eyes.

That took the steam out of Martha's sails. "Well, no. I mean, I did get some messages, but I never stayed in one place too long and I seem to get everything so messed up," she panted. "I thought it best to just show on up and see what gives."

I shook my head and struggled to my feet with El's help. "How did you find me?"

"I was pulled over for speeding and when I told the sheriff who I was, he gave me an escort."

"Really? That was kind of him." I looked over Martha's shoulder and sure enough the sheriff was taking in the scene with much amusement. I nodded and ignored him.

"Well, what you waiting for? Come on in," El suggested.

I rolled my eyes at this point. I wasn't so sure I wanted Martha in my trailer. It looked like she had all her stuff packed into her wagon as it was.

"No sense staying out here and being gawked

at." I gave the sheriff a quick wave of the hand and led the way inside.

Martha's eyes widened as she walked inside. "Mom, I had no idea we had such similar tastes."

El snorted. "Really? Purple is your favorite color too?"

Martha swung her hips. "What can I say? I like it wild and loud."

I about swallowed my tongue and changed the subject. "What happened to your husband?"

"Mom, that is a long story and I don't think you wanna hear all the messy details." Her eyes darted toward Eleanor.

"I do," El said. "I love juicy details." She rubbed her hands together.

I rolled my eyes at that. "If Martha doesn't care to tell me she doesn't have to."

"Don't listen to her. Get it off your chest, Martha." El proceeded to pour coffee into a cup and offered it to Martha. "Don't spare any details. As you might imagine, it would be quite hard to shock me."

"That much is true, El, but I barely survived your stories." I nudged El to hush. I really didn't want to hear it, and something told me it was going to be more information than I cared to know.

Martha hunkered down on the hot pink couch, feeling the fabric for Lord knows what reason. "Well, my husband, Johnny West, was what you'd call pretty straight-laced. Preacher of a Baptist church if you can believe that."

"I recall that much," I said.

Martha poured creamer into her coffee while under the watchful eye of both El and I.

"Yup, she's your daughter all right."

"I've never known Mom to even drink coffee."

"You also haven't seen me in ten years. When you dropped Sophia off for the summer, you high-tailed it out of here so quick I would have thought the devil was chasing you."

"I'm awful sorry about that, but my life was pretty chaotic back then."

"Unlike now, I suppose."

Ignoring the barb, she said, "Like I was saying, after I married Johnny, I got pregnant with Sophia real quick-like and he wasn't too happy about that one. For all appearances-sake he was a model husband."

"Aren't they all," El laughed.

"You got that one right, old girl. Preacher man had roaming hands."

"There seems to be a lot of that going around. So what did you do?" El asked, obviously trying to extract every seedy detail.

"Not much I could do," she sighed. "I tried my best to act the part of dutiful wife and mother. I focused myself on raising Sophia the best I could, but truth be known, I hated all that fire and brimstone preaching."

"Plus, it was based on a lie," I added.

"Yes, one of the reasons I sent Sophia to spend the summers with you. I knew you'd be a good influence on her."

"Thanks. I really enjoyed those summers with Sophia." I wiped a tear away thinking about all the days with Sophia on the beach, gardening and fishing.

El leaned forward. "Are you still married to the no good son of a—"

"El!" I shouted. "That's none of our business."

"When Sophia left for college, the whole cheating business hit the airwaves. We divorced not long afterward, and I just high-tailed it out of there." She frowned. "I knew I should have told you what was going on, but I was in my own private hell. I went down to South America and did some missionary work for awhile, but I met another roaming hand man down there that had a mind to put me into the missionary position, so I left back to the states."

"Some men," El gasped. "So what did you do then? For money, I mean?"

I gritted my teeth. "El, please leave this alone."

"Aggie, it's not like I was asking her if she was a hooker!" El laughed. "Nothing wrong with being a hooker. Why back in the day—"

"You're so incorrigible, El." I turned to Martha. "She's just kidding."

Martha continued on. "I just roamed from town to town. Most resorts will hire you and give you room and board." She paused. "I got back in touch with a few friends and they told me about Sophia and that you left numerous messages."

"So you weren't aware that your daughter was even missing for a whole year?" El asked in astonishment.

"No. Well, I-I left right after she went off to college."

I narrowed my eyes. It was not the reaction I was expecting. "I'm not sure what to make of this story."

"So I'm not the best mom on the planet. You have me there, but it's not all been on my end, you know. Sophia was quite upset when her father and I divorced, you see."

I folded my arms across my chest and took the role of a disappointed mother. "I wish I could see. Truth is that Sophia never mentioned anything about the divorce. If there was one, that is."

"Think what you like. Do you know how I can find her? I think it's time I reconnected with my little girl."

"She's no girl anymore, she's a woman. And I'll have to run this by her before I give you any info."

She gasped. "Thanks a lot!"

"You just can't show up on someone's door after all these years and expect to be welcomed with open arms."

I opened the door just then as Duchess came up to the door. When the door closed, I saw that Duchess had something in her mouth. Another dang mouse! "Duchess, don't you dare let that thing loose in here." She looked up at me, defiance in her eyes, and promptly placed it on the floor. I watched the mouse dart away and practically groaned. "I have half a mind to take you to the animal shelter." I shook a fist.

Duchess jumped up next to Martha who scurried to her feet. "I hate cats," Martha exclaimed. As if in response, Duchess hissed, her fur rose upward and her back arched.

Eleanor chuckled. "It looks like Duchess doesn't care much for you either."

I picked Duchess up and placed her before her food dish. She looked lazily up at me and tore into her food. "Poor dear. I promise to not neglect you so."

"So, where are you staying?" El asked Martha.

"I'm not sure yet. Maybe mosey off and see if they have an open spot here."

"Not in this campground?" I cleared my throat. "From the looks of it you don't have a camper and they don't allow tents here."

"I could rent a camper."

"You could rent a cabin down the road."

Martha frowned. "Okay, I get it. You just don't want me around."

"I-It's not that. I-I just..." I had to tell Sophia she was back in town before Martha showed up there unannounced, too.

El patted my hand. "It's all right, dear. I know this is the shock of your life." She turned toward Martha. "I'm afraid Aggie might need to adjust to you being in town, Martha."

Martha stood and made her way toward the door and we followed her outside. "I suppose it might be best if I head out now. I'll find suitable accommodations somewhere else."

We watched as she tore out down the gravel drive and I just shook. "Come on, El, before she tracks down Sophia."

We hopped back into the Caddy and zoomed down the street toward Sophia's apartment. She lived in a duplex on the northern edge of East Tawas. It wasn't on the lake but across the road where the woods bordered the property. When we pulled up Sophia was outside talking with Trooper Sales who was wearing the same clothes he had on last night!

We walked toward the pair. "Aggie, just settle yourself down," El said.

I turned to glare at her, "Meaning?"

El grimaced with a curve to her lips. "If looks could kill, Sales would be dead."

"I like Sales. I just don't like him near my granddaughter."

Eleanor gasped. "Everybody needs somebody."

I wasn't about to be swayed. "He needs to find himself a woman his own age."

"Shucks, Aggie, he can't be all that older than she is."

Sophia eyes widened and Sales turned. "Gramms, what are you doing here?"

Sales smiled weakly. "I best get going and let you two talk. I'm working today."

As he jumped into his truck I said, "You might want to go home and change clothes first. You know how rumor mills are around here. I'd hate for my granddaughter's reputation to be flawed in any way."

"Would it matter if I told you I slept on the couch?"

I ignored him and hugged Sophia, and after a full minute, Sales spun off down the road.

"Gramms, I c-can't breathe."

"I'm so sorry." I wiped at a tear in my eye. "I have something to tell you."

Sophia's pallor whitened. "You make it sound so bad. Did somebody die?"

I shook my head as Sophia led us inside. Sophia's place was quite small and I noted the blanket and pillows on her blue sofa. Maybe the trooper really did sleep on the couch. Not that it mattered at the moment.

Along one wall were family pictures including, one with Eleanor sticking her tongue out. There were also many I had taken of Sophia on her yearly vacations to Tawas. No pictures of either Martha or her father Johnny. Not having one single picture of your parents couldn't be a good thing, although I doubted Martha had one of me either.

Sophia rattled in the kitchen and soon the smell of coffee hung thickly in the air. Her kitchen consisted of an open floor plan with white cupboards. You'd be hard pressed to make much of a meal in that small a kitchen. When the coffee was done, she brought us each a cup with my favorite vanilla creamer. "I wish I knew just how to say this."

Sophia wrinkled her brow. "Say what?"

"When is the last time you heard from your mom?" I asked as I poured the creamer.

Her eyes widened. "I-I d-don't remember exactly, maybe since before college."

"Not since last summer?"

"No. I mean, I did try and call her, but Martha doesn't have a phone."

"Martha?" I was a little taken aback by Sophia referencing her as Martha, not mom.

"I know she's my mom and all, but she hasn't been much of one in many years. Not since the divorce, anyway."

"I see. And she just fell off the planet and you never noticed?"

"I had more important things on my plate, like school." She tugged a brush through her hair. "She hasn't contacted you?"

"We had a strained relationship. I haven't really spoken much to her. She'd drop you off in the summer when you were a child and left real fast like. I can't recall the last time we had more than a few words spoken between us." I cleared my throat. "I did try and call her last summer, but she never returned my phone calls either."

Sophia circled her finger around the coffee cup. "There was a neighbor's phone number, but after the divorce, she just took off and I haven't heard from her since."

"How about your dad?"

"He remarried and moved to Florida." She frowned. "I don't hear from him and I quit calling."

"I'm so sorry, Sophia. I just don't get it. I don't understand what would make Martha behave that way. I certainly didn't raise her that way."

"It's not your fault, Gramms."

Eleanor smiled sympathetically. "It's a good thing you two have each other."

"Thanks, Eleanor. Who wouldn't like spending time with the most awesome Gramms ever?" She smiled. "So what is the big news?"

I coughed at that. "Martha is in town. She dropped by my campsite."

Sophia's mouth gaped open and she swallowed hard. "I see. You didn't tell her where I live, did you?"

"Of course not! But she said that she wanted to find you. I'm afraid it will only be a matter of time. I'm as uncomfortable as you are about this whole deal."

"Was she alone?"

"Yes, why?"

With a faraway look in her eye, she said, "Just curious, I guess."

I gave Sophia a quick hug again. "I didn't want this to be a shock to you if she turns up is all."

I moved away as Eleanor answered her cell phone. She nodded as I mouthed, "Who is it?" Holding up a finger in pause, she said, "Thanks, we'll be there shortly," and powered off the phone.

"Who was that?"

"Another tip. It seems there is a court hearing happening that has something to do with Herman Butler's remains."

"Just like the sheriff mentioned last night."

"Yup, maybe he's turning over a new leaf."

"Maybe. Is the widow pushing for the cremation?"

El nodded her head. "Sounds that way."

"You two better get on over there, then," Sophia said. "I need to get ready for work."

El and I rushed out the door and raced over to the courthouse like folks half our age. "Strange how we can move fast-like when in the midst of a case," I said.

"I wouldn't miss this for the world," El replied. "Maybe that hunk of man funeral director will be there."

"Why shouldn't that surprise me?"

"I need to upsize."

"He looks a little super-sized."

"At least I won't have to worry about hurting him, then." she chuckled.

"Please don't elaborate. I don't think my breakfast settled yet. That or the activities of this morning just haven't resonated with me yet. What with Martha showing up and Sophia's reaction to the news, it's all a little too much and too soon."

CHAPTER TWELVE

When El and I arrived at the courthouse the parking lot was packed, but I managed to squeeze into a space, maybe a bit too close between cars.

Eleanor went to chuckling, her belly doing flip flops. "There is no way I can squeeze out, Aggie, just no way."

"Sorry."

I backed out enough so she could get out and I then drove back into the space. I managed to squeeze out of the car and between them to where Eleanor stood, but I had to suck in my gut like crazy.

With a joking observation, I said, "I'm impressed." Eleanor winked.

"You should be. I snagged my ass on the rear bumper I think." I rubbed the area and felt my torn pants. "Oh my, I have ripped my pants!"

El motioned me to turn and when I did, she gasped. "How are you planning to go in there with your grannies showing."

"Those are from Victoria's Secret, I'll have you know."

El rolled her eyes. "I wish they sold them in my size."

We made our way toward the single story brick building that contained the Iosco County Court House, covering my torn pants with my purse.

We walked inside and my eyes peeled to the deputies. I froze and swallowed hard. "I hope you don't have your pistol with you, old girl," I whispered to El.

"Nope. I know better than that!"

"Move along!" a female deputy shouted. The woman looked at us suspiciously as she said, "Place your purses on the conveyor belt and walk through the metal detector."

"No need to be rude, dear," I said. *These people are playing hardball.* I can't blame them. It was a sign of the times.

I placed my purse on the conveyor belt and walked through the metal detector, ignoring the snickers from the deputy on the other side. Obviously they had noted my ripped apparel. I grabbed my purse and held it behind me as I waited for El's turn.

When she trounced through the machine, lights and sirens sounded.

"Go back through!" the deputy shouted.

She complied, but not without a few words. "It's that bullet that is lodged in my butt. Been there since Nam."

I wanted to slap her just now. *Why can't she be serious? This is no joking matter.*

"Empty your pockets."

She pulled out a roll of quarters from her pocket, placed them into the tray, and walked back through. The alarms sounding yet again.

"Jesus." Eleanor reached into her bra and guns were drawn by the deputies.

"Freeze!"

El stood with her hands raised. "It's just my cellphone."

"She keeps it in her bra," I replied.

"You can take it out yourself if you'd like," El said, licking her lips.

Sheriff Peterson walked toward us with quite the scowl. "You two can't do anything without causing a ruckus."

I shrugged while El's eyes focused on the ceiling.

Guns were put away and the sheriff gave the trio of deputies a nod of approval. I gaped in shock; they deserved a verbal tongue lashing in my opinion for pulling a gun on defenseless senior citizens like us. *What nerve!*

El joined me, setting no further alarms off. She retrieved her cellphone and put it back in her bra with a wink in the deputy's direction.

"Show off," I said.

El pranced off, ignoring the barb. We were escorted to the district courtroom where the hearing was taking place. We crept to the front bench behind the widow, well within earshot of the proceedings.

Judge Gayle McDonald sat on the raised bench, her heavy framed glasses resting on the bridge of her nose. "It's my understanding that this is in regards to your late husband's remains. A Mr Herman Butler?"

"Yes, Your Honor," Betty Lou Butler replied.

She was dressed in a cream-colored business suit with skirt. Her hair was even brighter than it was when we saw her last night at the Hidden Cove.

"What is your objection to the funeral, exactly?"

"I want him cremated, but some Butler Foundation says that's not possible." She laughed nervously. "He was my husband. He was not married to the Butler Foundation."

There were deep furrows that appeared in the judge's brow. "When did you get married?"

"The day before he died."

"There is a pending investigation, Your Honor," a lawyer across the room stated.

"That has no bearing over this case unless Herman Butler's remains haven't been released yet by the medical examiner." She cleared her throat. "Well, have they?"

"No, and we plan to file paperwork that is related to this case." He took a sip of water.

"Related to the means of burial?"

"Yes, Your Honor," the lawyer stated. "It's unclear if Mrs. Butler is aware of the type of inheritance that was involved with the Butler Mansion."

Glancing from behind her glasses, the judge said, "And what prevented you from filing the paperwork?"

The lawyer pulled at his shirt collar.

"May I please approach the bench, Your Honor?" a voice asked from the front bench behind the nervous lawyer.

"And you are who?"

"Andrew Hart."

Andrew stood dressed in a blue suit that hugged his body like an embrace. *Wishful thinking on my part*, I thought. I wished a few more things, but that's not possible with Andrew's availability up to question.

"Are you part of the legal team?"

"I am an interested party. I represent Herman Butler's daughter."

"You may approach."

He approached with the stuttering lawyer and Betty Lou who, from the looks of it, was representing herself. *What is that saying about having a fool for a client?*

"I can't hear anything," Eleanor whispered.

"I think that's the point." I put a finger near my lips. The last thing I wanted was to be booted from court.

The trio moved back to where they were before and waited as the judge took her glasses off. "There is yet another cross-complaint in this case and it's with a heavy heart that I must adjourn this matter until this afternoon, two o'clock." She took a drink of water from a glass on the bench."

"Cremation," Betty Lou reminded her.

"I'm here to carry out the law, Mrs. Butler, not make judgment calls," the judge replied. "I'm not sure why you didn't retain a lawyer, Mrs. Butler, but I'm sure you were advised to do so when you filed."

The judge slammed the gavel down to signify the adjournment of court, retreating to her chambers. Eleanor and I waited while the courtroom cleared and as Andrew passed us by, he winked.

My heart fluttered. "Oh, my."

"Not the actions of an uninterested man," El observed.

"I wonder..."

We walked out and decided to stay put for the time being as cars filed out of the lot. When a fair amount had, we made our way and were stopped by a beaming Andrew.

"You two up for lunch?"

"I-I—"

"Sure, but Aggie ripped her pants earlier and needs to go to the campground and get fresh clothes."

I had to bite my tongue. *Fresh, indeed.*

"Campground?" Andrew asked. "You're still there?"

"Why would you think otherwise?"

"They sure are slow at rebuilding your house."

"It's not been that long since you left town, remember?"

"I do, believe me. I remember it well."

He eyed me suggestively to which I sighed. "Okay, so where do we meet you for lunch?"

"Not at Kentucky Fried Chicken, I hope," Eleanor laughed.

"Good times," Andrew laughed. "How about the Whitetail Café?"

"We'll meet you there."

"Can I ride with you, Andrew?" Eleanor asked. "You can meet us there once you get changed. Okay, Aggie?"

"Whatever."

I walked away and thankfully, the car parked on the driver's side was gone. I hopped in and drove home changing into white pants and a button up shirt, sliding my feet into white pumps.

Since Andrew had left town, I felt like the wind

had been sucked out of my sails. It's embarrassing to say I even let myself go. I quit monitoring my diet and put on a good ten pounds. Not something that I'm proud of, mind you. Gaining weight at my age just wasn't a good thing. It's hard enough for me to do the occasional walk around the campground, something I enjoyed until witch lady parked across from me that is. My hip was an ever-present reminder that I'm no spring chicken. I knew that, but I'm not ready to accept inactivity any time soon or orthopedic surgery.

I arrived at the Whitetail Café ten minutes later. There was a whitetail deer head painted on the plate glass window. As I strolled inside, I found Andrew and El easily enough as it was a small place.

I cleared my throat, but Eleanor didn't move. Obviously she was content with sitting across from Andrew.

Andrew smiled, patting the chair next to him. I opted to sit next to Eleanor instead. His eyes met mine and I wiped my sweaty palms on my slacks. My chest ached, too. I breathed deeply of the cologne that Andrew wore. Why, that alone would send any woman to swoon. I'm so glad I'm not that *type of woman* or I could be if he showed the least bit of interest. If he wasn't married, that is.

"That didn't take long."

Eleanor snickered. "She's a fast dresser."

"She's fast when she gets undressed," Andrew added.

I about choked. "I don't think I like where this is going." I was suddenly hot all over like I was having a hot flash, something I hadn't had for years.

"No?" Andrew positively beamed.

Changing the subject, I said, "So, Herman Butler has a daughter?"

"Yes, and I'd rather not talk about this right now."

I eyeballed him. "And why is that?"

"Because I promised her I would conduct this case with some discretion."

"So, I guess this means you haven't filed the paperwork yet. But I still wonder why she wouldn't want to show in court."

"Why are you giving me a hard time here?" he laughed.

"I-I d-don't know.

I had hoped to do a real investigation here and it seems like if they cremate Herman Butler it's a crap shoot to prove he may have died under mysterious circumstances."

"It's mysterious, all right," Eleanor said. "Like how did Betty Lou fit him through the window?"

"I meant if foul play was at hand."

Andrew nodded. "Seems like a good call on your part, Aggie."

"You'd think she'd have stayed married a bit longer before she decided to off her husband though," I added.

Andrew rubbed his chin, and just then, a young man approached and set an iced tea down, promising our food would soon be ready. "Hey wait, do you still make those delicious chocolate shakes with whipped cream?"

"We sure do."

"Then bring one for the lady here." He smiled. "Your favorite, if I recall correctly," Andrew said.

I squirmed uncomfortably in my seat. "Thanks, Andrew." I touched his arm for a second and yanked it back like it was on fire. *It sure lit one inside of me.*

I yawned, taking a sip of tea while I awaited the shake. I hoped it would rejuvenate me. "I wish there was some way we could get them to do an autopsy."

"That is strange, indeed. I wonder how they expect to find a cause of death without one."

"Exactly my point." I leaned forward. "Oh, you didn't know that tidbit of info, Andrew? I thought your client should have that information seeing as how she's Herman's daughter." I smiled smugly.

"He has a wife, or did you forget? She's more privy to information than my client."

I leaned forward. "I heard Betty Lou was locked out of the mansion."

Andrew took a sip of water and then answered. "Really? By whom?"

"I'm unclear right now, but it wasn't the sheriff."

"Hmm, that's odd. The Butler Foundation hired Mr. Simpleton."

I cracked a smile at that. "Mr. Simpleton?"

"The other lawyer at court today."

Eleanor rubbed her hands together. "Wow, now the plot thickens."

I sighed. "I don't understand why the Butler Foundation is so insistent that Herman be buried at the family cemetery."

"Or that they would lock the widow out of the house," Eleanor added. "If they were responsible, that is."

I leaned forward. "El's right. How does the Butler Foundation have the power to oust the widow, and so quickly?"

"All good questions. I see you two are headed in the right direction."

Our food was set down and the young man disappeared back to the kitchen. I stared down at my hamburger and French fries and realized there was no ketchup. Before I had a chance to react, Andrew grabbed one from the next table and handed it to me. I sipped my chocolate shake and licked the whipped cream from my lips before saying, "Thanks."

Eleanor said between bites of her tacos, "It's a setup."

I shrugged. "Peterson isn't worried so what can we do?"

Andrew's face tightened. "So Peterson is up to the same ole thing then?"

"He says he's keeping an eye on her."

"Maybe he is. Why else would he be at Hidden Cove last night?" Eleanor asked.

"Except for the fact he goes there every Wednesday. I wonder why?"

Andrew arched a brow. "Trouble at home perhaps?"

"Hopefully not. Aggie sent Stacey to distract him. I'd hate to think his wife found out he was hanging out with the wax queen."

I glared at her but before I could say anything ...

"Wax queen?" Andrew asked. "I'd rather not know the details. I'd hate to be an accessory."

"You're guilty by association."

"You're probably right, old girl," he winked.

I wasn't sure, but knowing Peterson the way I did, I'm just not inclined to believe he would change his tune this quick. We were not what you'd call friends or even allies.

We ate our food and returned to the courthouse

and this time we sat in the front. We all stood as Judge McDonald entered the courtroom and sat down behind the bench.

I felt a little catch in my throat when she spoke. "I'm recessing until Monday morning."

"But that's in three days!" Betty Lou shouted.

"Mrs. Butler, no more outbursts in court or you'll be cooling your heels in jail for the weekend."

Betty Lou gingerly lifted her index finger.

"You may speak."

"Will this put off the funeral?"

"I can't imagine how this might seem to you, but this is how the law works, Mrs. Butler. I'm allowing the attorney until Monday to have the necessary paperwork or I will be dismissing this case." She lowered the gavel and we filed out of court.

As we left, I spotted Andrew talking to the other attorney and that mystery woman! I stormed past and El caught up with me outside. "Would you wait up, Aggie? I'm an old woman, don't ya know."

I whirled. "I'm old, too. Maybe a little too old for this kind of ruse."

Eleanor still panting, "Ruse?"

"Yes, Andrew is playing hot and cold. He winks at me, but he's with her!"

I stomped away with Eleanor hot on my heels.

"He doesn't act like a man involved with another woman, and he might not be."

We arrived at the Caddy and within minutes, I barreled out of there like the devil was chasing me.

CHAPTER THIRTEEN

I gripped the steering wheel as I drove, trying not to think about Andrew and *that woman*! After lunch it was really too much. There he was all acting so damn flirtatious and I was sucking it up like a fool.

Eleanor interrupted my dark thought pattern. "You need to just ask him outright if he's involved with another woman."

I groaned. She knew me too well. "I'm not doing that! Geez, El, I know when a man isn't interested."

El chuckled. "He looks interested, all right. Maybe we should find out who that woman is."

"Maybe we should find out who and what the Butler Foundation is?"

"They contribute quite a bit to the community."

"So does every other crook," I pointed out.

El fanned herself. "Aggie, you need to cool down and get your bearings, like where do we go from here?"

My bearings, huh? "I just want to go back

home and relax before sundown." I smiled with devilish intent.

"Why sundown?"

"Because we're gonna be doing a little investigating."

She giggled. "Like where?"

"I'd love to get into the Butler Mansion."

El rubbed her hands together. "Or take a look around the cemetery."

"I dare say we'd break a leg out there in the dark."

"How we gonna get in the Butler Mansion? Somebody has to be living there."

"Why don't you buzz your maid friend and get the low down."

El's raised her voice an octave. "Oh, I don't know. She might not want to get involved further."

"Why not? She was the one who called us to begin with."

"When folks turn up dead, things can get mighty tense. She might be under investigation, too. She was there that night too, you know."

I made the turn and parked in my camping site. When we were walking inside, loud music was blaring from Leotyne's campsite. Eleanor waved at her and received a wave back. In her hand, she held a blood red wineglass. I thought it might be a good time to make peace with my new neighbor, so I strolled over there.

I put my hand out. "I'm Agnes Barton."

She pointed her finger in my face. "The devil w-will s-see y-you soon," she sung.

My teeth chattered and as I turned the other cheek—tripped over a log—and knocked over a pot that was cooking over the campfire. I whirled and stood helpless as flames shot across the grass, and caught the fabric Leotyne had draped across her camper. I waved my arms frantically. "Watch out, Leotyne!"

"Oh shit." Eleanor ran around in circles. "Look what you did. Somebody call 911!"

Leotyne screeched, waving her hands in the air as I looked for something to put the fire out with.

"Stop it, Eleanor! Get something to put out the fire!"

Minutes later, I grabbed my sun tea and threw it on the flames.

"We need more sun tea!" El exclaimed. "Where is the fire department when you need them?"

It seemed like hours before they did show up, which might have only been fifteen minutes later as we so busy throwing whatever type of liquid on the fire that wasn't flammable. All the while, Leotyne bellowed bloody murder. Sure, a few fellow campers helped out, but the majority just watched from a comfortable distance.

Suddenly we were propelled backward as a fire hose sprayed across the camper, extinguishing the flames. *Finally*, I thought as we were pounded to the ground.

El and I were both wet as drowned rats and were lying in a mud puddle created by the water from the hose. I struggled up and just then, a flash went off.

"This will be great front page material," a girl's voice bellowed. The teenager batted her eyelashes at the firefighter, Curtis, who for lack of a better word had no clue he was calendar ready.

"If I was ten years younger, I'd be calling in false alarms all the time," I whispered to Eleanor.

From behind cupped hands, El said, "They can charge you for that sort of thing."

"Sorry ladies," Curtis called over.

We shrugged like it happened all the time just as Peterson trudged in our direction, glancing first at us and then the gypsy's trailer. "Should I even ask?" He slapped his hand across his face. "So much for me getting home early today."

"That is just too bad," I said. "Things happen and you just have to deal with it." I curtly nodded in his direction.

Leotyne raced forward screaming, "That woman," as she pointed her scrawny finger in my face, "set my trailer on fire!"

My hands went to my hips. "I did no such thing."

Eleanor bit her lip. "You kinda did, Aggie."

I turned on her. "W-Well I didn't mean to," I pleaded with the sheriff. "It was just an accident. If that witch there hadn't been singing her devil songs to me, I'd have never knocked over that pot!" I gasped.

"It was pretty funny, though," El laughed and then bit her lip when I glared at her.

"Some sidekick you are." My eyes went to slits now. "I have a mind to never speak to you again."

"I have a half a mind to haul you off to jail to sort this out," Sheriff Peterson said.

"No, you just have half a mind. She was singing 'the devil would see me soon'. Isn't there a law against putting curses on folks?"

"No, I don't believe there is," he smirked.

"How was I supposed to know that the fire could spread so fast? All I did was knock a pot over. It only caught the fabric on her trailer and was put out rather quickly."

"Yes, well we haven't gotten near enough rain this year," Peterson reminded me.

"That's true, Aggie." Eleanor nodded her head like some kind of bobble head.

"Sheriff, if you want to haul me off, go ahead, but I swear it was an accident."

"I'm not doing that," he hissed. "I was just trying to scare you."

El's face got real white. "You shouldn't do that. Don't you know Aggie is a frail old woman?" She slapped her chest. "Her ticker isn't all that good."

"She's like a ticking time bomb."

I winced and sat on the picnic table while the fire truck whirled away. Peterson was there quite a while taking the report and talking to a variety of witnesses, none of whom could remember how the fire started. Eleanor was playing dumb. I sighed in relief at that. I understand the man is just doing his job, but I hoped this escapade wouldn't land me in jail! Our personalities sure clash!

CHAPTER FOURTEEN

When Peterson left, I staggered into my camper where I retrieved my shower supplies and traipsed to the campground shower. I was in a dark mood and very irritated that Eleanor couldn't shut her mouth. I had no clue if she had left for home or not. The spray of the water did little to relieve the pain as my hip had begun to throb. I'm fairly certain it was because of the fall to the ground El and I took.

Afterward, I stood in front of the mirror and tried to get my hair into some kind of order. "What is wrong with you, Agnes Barton?" I asked out loud. For once in my life, I wanted something I couldn't have. Andrew. It was just like the old days when I worked for him, but he was married then. Problem was that he had promised to come back to town, but never called when he was back.

I wore a denim dress that was well above the knees, but who cares ... *not me*. I limped back to my campsite and just like I figured the manager, Henry, was waiting for me. El's Caddy was nowhere in sight either, to which I frowned. I hadn't meant to get harsh with her.

"Agnes?" Henry shuffled his feet. "I know the fire wasn't your fault and all, but you need to cool it, okay? I'd hate to put you out of the campground." With nothing more to say, he walked back to his office.

I went inside and passed out on the bed with the sound of Duchess purring me to sleep. It was quite a bit later before I woke to a terrible scratching sound. I went to see what was happening. Duchess was batting the mouse around, jumping over the table and countertop in her excitement, sending paper cups and chips tumbling to the floor. "Stop it, you crazy cat." I shook my balled fist at her.

I vowed first thing tomorrow to see about the construction of my house. I wasn't sure how much longer I could tolerate living in cramped quarters.

I glanced outside and nearly had a heart attack as Eleanor had her hands cupped, looking in my window. When I opened the door, Eleanor moved past me carrying two large bags.

I smiled. "I smell Chinese food."

"I thought you might be ready for a treat." She frowned. "You still mad at me?"

"Me? Mad at you? That would be a complete waste of time."

Eleanor scanned my clothing. "I don't think I have ever seen you in denim before. It suits you."

Eleanor wore black shorts and shirt, a stark contrast to her fair skin.

"Are we going somewhere?"

With fingers curved into claws, she said, "I thought we were planning to check out the Butler Mansion?"

"I'm not sure I'm up to it. My hip's hurting."

El belched and giggled. "Oops, sorry. We can do a drive by at least, can't we?"

"Drive by? I love you El, but I'm not going to prison with you. I'm too old to be someone's bitch."

She nearly fell off the couch at that. "No, you'd be running the show."

"Not so sure about that one. It seems like you're more in control than me lately. What gives?" I took a bite of my egg roll.

"Not much to tell. My nemesis is out of town for the whole month."

"No Dorothy Alton to raise your blood pressure or get into daily fist fights. It's going to be one boring summer." I snapped the tab of my Diet Coke. "How about in the man department?"

She slurped her Coke and as it dripped to her chin, I handed her a napkin. "I'm working on it. How about you?"

I waved my hand. "I gave up on that." I forked

in a mouthful of orange chicken. "Don't even mention Andrew. That's a done deal."

"Done how?"

"I'm over him and his crap!"

"I'm good with that, but you might be interested to know that—"

I pounded my fists on the table. "I don't want to talk about him anymore."

"Fine, fine, but Agnes Barton, you're the most stubborn woman I have ever known."

"So are you," I laughed. "I can be, but it's all with good reason."

"Agnes Barton's way."

A knock at the door interrupted us. When El whipped the door open, Teresa, the maid from the Butler Mansion stood there. She was as pale as a ghost and trembling something fierce.

"Come in, dear," El said.

She walked in and took a seat. "The house is real empty now, but I still work there." She glanced at her shoes briefly. "It kills me to know that dust is gathering and I'm locked out."

"Who ordered the lockout?"

"The state police. Not even the Butler Foundation has access right now."

My eyes swept over her. "And how would you know?"

"Word travels fast in a small town."

I nodded, glancing over the sweat beading

on Teresa's brow. "I bet. So, what did you come here for? I'm guessing it wasn't to discuss dust or the foundation."

She glanced up. "My, no, it's just that I went out to get some cleaning supplies and drove by the mansion and..." She began to cry. "You know, just to see if the tape had been removed and I found a body on the ground."

I leaned forward. "Who is it?"

"I-I'm not sure, I was so scared that I came straight here." She trembled.

We jumped to our feet. "Did you call the police?" El asked.

She shook her head. "I-I came here first. I just don't know what to do."

"We better call 911 right away," I said. "Sheriff Peterson wasn't too happy when we didn't call right away before."

"Oh, he's never happy," Eleanor scoffed. "But you're right, Agnes."

"Still, I wonder..."

Eleanor's eyes practically glowed. "We could call him on the way, like from the driveway."

"That's a killer idea." *Oops, maybe not the best choice of words*, I thought.

We hustled out the door and followed Teresa back to the Butler Mansion where we left our vehicles beside the driveway and walked towards the house as Eleanor called 911.

It was dark now with a little light reflecting off the roof from the yard lights, but it didn't quite illuminate the area where the body lay. It was hard to determine the sex or age of the dark shape sprawled on the ground.

I turned to Teresa. "Do you have a flashlight?"

Teresa shrugged, "Well, no."

"Shine the headlights on the body, Aggie," Eleanor suggested.

"Great idea, El." I positioned the car directly facing the body on the ground and hurried back to El and Teresa.

"That's Earl Perkins!" Teresa shouted. "He's worked here for...like forever."

"Really?" I said.

"Yes. He also works as a gravedigger," Teresa added.

I took a step back. "You mean for the cemetery here?"

"Among others. Smaller cemeteries still dig them by hand."

"Yuck," Eleanor sneered. "I'm all for cremation."

"Really? That's good to know. As for me I just want to be buried right next to my husband at Forest Lawn in Saginaw, Michigan. It's right near where Mr. Burt's Mausoleum is."

"Who is Mr. Burt?" Teresa asked.

"Wellington Burt was a lumber baron and

was the eighth richest man in America a century ago." I took in a breath. "He may have also been the stingiest as he didn't leave his family a dime of his fortune."

"He had one humdinger of a will," El cut in.

"The will didn't pay his descendants a dime until twenty-one years after his last living grandchild had died. That's every living relative he had at the time." I smiled in the darkness. "I might as well tell you what I think is an interesting story seeing as how I can't see a thing."

"That is one tough cookie," Teresa said. "Some men have some peculiar wills."

"Ain't that the truth," El agreed.

"The Butler's had a strange will too," she began. "It seems that only a true Butler relative can inherit the fortune, but if none exist, the Butler Foundation inherits everything.

"Fortune," El gasped. "You mean..."

"Not just the mansion," I cut in?

"Nope, they were in shipping, big. It seems that married to a Butler isn't enough. When Herman inherited the fortune, he signed a clause which bars his wife from inheriting a dime."

"And the mansion?" I asked.

"She can't lay claim to that, either."

"Was there also a clause stating that he had to be buried on the property, too?"

"Yup."

"This is one humdinger of a will," El said.

I did wonder about Herman's daughter, but for some reason I held back. Perhaps it was the body that laid here on the ground, or the breeze that blew suddenly, as if without warning.

Just then, lights lit up to where we stood as the sheriff's car and three state police cruisers raced forward with lights flashing.

We were like deer in headlights. In fact, I think I saw a few dart away at their approach.

Trooper Sales led the pack as a spotlight lit up the area where the body lay. The man's neck was bent at an odd angle ... *just like Herman Butler.* I gazed up at the gloomy mansion and gulped hard. The body lay in the same approximate area where Herman Butler's body was discovered.

"Who called?" Trooper Sales asked.

"I did," Eleanor said. "Teresa here found the grave digger dead."

"That's Earl Perkins on the ground there," I said. "Poor Teresa was so upset that she came to tell us and we called 911 en route."

"That's good and all, but, Miss, you do know you should call the police first," Sheriff Peterson said in an authoritative tone.

"She was scared to death, poor dear," I countered. "It's dark out already and she's all alone out here."

"Yeah, Sheriff. You can't blame the maid for panicking!" El shouted.

"That's enough. The boys from the crime lab will be here soon," Peterson said.

I shivered myself. Two dead bodies was two too many, in my opinion.

"I'm afraid, Agnes and Eleanor, you will need to give us an official statement," Peterson said.

"I already told you, Teresa came to the campground and told us she found a body on the property."

"And we came to check it out," El added.

"And it was here just like she said. Teresa can tell you the rest." I swiped at my brow. "I personally don't know the man." I turned to face Eleanor. "How about you, El?"

"I know he works out at the Butler Mansion, but that's all."

"I see," Sales said. As he faced Teresa, she began to cry. "Why were you here when police tape is all over the place?"

"I just wondered if it had been removed is all."

I put a finger in the air, "And about that, Sales? Why is police tape in place? I thought the medical examiner decided not to do an autopsy."

"I know, but the state police is still investigating."

"That's not what Sheriff Peterson said."

"Not reading your emails again, Peterson?" Sales asked.

"Oh darn, it must be in the spam folder," he

joked. "Actually, I believe what I said was the sheriff's department wasn't investigating."

"Laugh it up, Sheriff. It's not like we don't have another body to contend with," I spat.

Peterson got really serious, sort of, "We could flip a coin on who gets to file the report."

"He's joking," Sales said. "We'll both be here for the remainder of the night most likely." To which the sheriff grumbled, "Go on home ladies. We'll be in touch, but I hope I won't see you any sooner than the next police fundraiser."

I whirled at that. "I sure hope you make damn sure an autopsy is performed this time."

"Go on home and let us do our jobs, Agnes," Sales said.

"Do you mind if we check out the inside of the mansion before we leave"? I asked.

"Not happening, Agnes. You should know better than that by now," Peterson snapped.

"I know, I know, but I'm staying until..."

Peterson stepped forward. "No, you're leaving now or I'll be placing you under arrest."

"That won't go well with your superiors."

"Don't think for a minute they will supersede my decisions, so you might want to do what you're told this time." He paused. "I'd hate to see you to lose your gun permit."

I gasped at that. *I bet!* "We'll go, but I'm doing so under protest," I huffed.

"Should I take that as a sign of your compliance?"

El and I turned as we heard Teresa speak. "Betty Lou and the G.A.S.P. were here earlier in the day."

I ran forward. "Why didn't you say that before?"

"W-Well, it just occurred to me," Teresa whined.

"I'm sorry, dear. Didn't mean to bite your head off."

"Well, there is a full moon tonight, Aggie," Eleanor pointed out.

I ignored El. "How do you know they were here?"

"Yes," Peterson asked. "How, considering the mansion is locked up."

"Well, I saw them fly out of the drive. They nearly ran into my car."

"And you were sure Betty Lou was in their van?"

"Agnes!" Peterson bellowed as his handcuffs slapped against each other.

El and I took a few steps back as a show we were really leaving, and Teresa finally said, "I'm sure she was in their van. She was sitting in the passenger seat."

"What time?" I pressed.

"I'm not sure. I-I didn't really look at the clock."

"Who is G.A.S.P?" Sales cut in.

"Ghost hunters," I said and continued on. "You weren't worried that the trio would somehow get inside the house?"

"No, the state police were real insistent that we were not to return until the investigation was over."

"A rule obviously you all ignored," Peterson pointed out.

"Did they drag Betty Lou bodily from the property?" I asked.

El cut in. "Yeah, don't seem like the widow would just up an leave like that, even if the fuzz told her to."

"True, El, she's fighting over the remains. Why not fight about being ousted if this house belonged to her late husband?"

"She didn't fuss much at all since none of us really had a choice," Teresa said.

"Are there any cameras on the premises?" I asked.

Teresa paused as in thought for a moment and then shook her head.

"Special locks?"

"Well, I did hear the Butler Foundation had changed the locks, with the state police's permission; of course, to secure the property."

"Do you know who the Butler Foundation is?"

"I'm not sure about who the members are, if that's what you're asking."

"Surely you met them before," I pressed. "Are you positive that—"

"I've had enough. Sales, do something about the busybodies or they'll be in the back of my squad car!" Peterson shouted.

"He's right, ladies. You can catch up with the maid at a later date."

"We'll be back!" Eleanor shouted.

El and I wandered back to the Caddy. "It just burns me to be interrupted just when I was getting somewhere."

We piled into the Caddy and passed the forensics van on our way back home.

"Teresa has placed Betty Lou at the crime scene at least earlier. I just wonder..."

El cleared her throat. "I just wished we had proof she was there."

"The maid said the locks had been changed."

"Still, Aggie, I wonder if Betty Lou somehow found a way inside?"

"Teresa never said, El, but that's a great question." I then shrugged. "If a body wants to get into a house, they will if they're sneaky enough."

"Like how?"

"Pick locks, breaking and entering, window left open." My hands tightened on the steering wheel. "Even though I can't see Betty Lou as a crawling through a window type."

El slapped her hands together, "One of G.A.S.P. could have done it."

I laughed at that with the mental image that conjured up. "True, Eleanor."

"And the Butler Foundation is starting to sound like goons," I said.

"True, Aggie," she shuddered.

"Butler Foundation, indeed," I said as I dimmed the high beams. "Are you familiar with them, El?"

"I know they're a charity organization, but the members never show up to any of their fundraisers."

"How is that?

"Apparently they set up the parties and hire all the help, but according to the newspaper they'd prefer to remain anonymous."

"Sounds like a bunch of crooks to me."

"Crooks that don't want Herman Butler cremated for some reason," El agreed.

My stomach growled. "Want to stop by Fuzzy's Ice Cream for a quick bite?"

El slapped her hands together. "That's the best idea so far."

CHAPTER FIFTEEN

I roared my way toward the nearest Fuzzy's that was located in Tadium, a short drive from Tawas. When we walked in, I was taken aback by the fact that both ghost hunters were here, and Betty Lou!

We shuffled in and sat down at our usual table as Sally Alton walked over. She wore shorts and a white Fuzzy's tee, her apron smeared with the colors of thirty-eight flavors, her blond hair pulled back into a tight braid.

She smiled in greeting. "It's kinda late for the two of you isn't it?"

I nodded. "We'll have the usual."

"One pineapple sundae with the works and a banana split for the champ over there," referring to Eleanor. Sally moved behind the counter, returning five minutes later with our delicious concoctions.

El laughed nervously. "I hear your grandparents are out of town."

She leaned in. "Are you missing my grandma, or your weekly fights?"

El scoffed. "Well ... I...."

I raised my hand. "Fights get my vote."

"How are you gonna get on the wall of shame if you don't have nobody to scrap with here?" Sally asked, motioning to the wall on the right.

Sure enough, there were pictures of Eleanor and Dorothy Alton in the midst of an ice cream fight. It looked like seniors gone wild because most if not all of the pictures were of senior-aged folks. Problem was you don't have to do too much to set the seniors off in this town. I smiled and knew I ranked up there, too. I just choose not to make them an ice cream-filled episode. I'd much rather eat ice cream than wear it.

I ate my pineapple sundae, keeping a watchful eye on Betty Lou and the boys from G.A.S.P. They were huddled together and spoke in hushed tones and that just wouldn't do for me.

I stood up and approached the trio. "Hello there, boys, Mrs. Butler." I gave her a curt nod. "I'm so sorry to hear about your troubles."

Eleanor gasped. "That must be awful having to postpone the funeral." She wiped at an invisible tear. "I dare say that would just be too much for me." She quivered.

Betty Lou looked up at us, her eyes more than a little red. Had she been drinking or was she really upset about her husband?

"Somehow I'm not feeling it, ladies," she said.

"I'm quite an investigator you know," I volunteered. "And is it also true that you were put out of your house?"

"Yes, you got that one right. When the law tells you they are locking the place up, you can't protest. I left at the time because I figured it was for the best, but now—I can't even dispose of my husband's remains. They told me it was just a matter of paperwork." She hung her head.

"What was, dear?"

"The house, I mean. He assured me things would be cleared up in a few days."

El spoke up. "Then they did the whole slap you with an order contesting the cremation, huh?"

She cried. "Yes. He's my husband, not theirs." She massaged her brow like it ached something fierce and I had half a mind to believe Betty Lou might be telling us the truth.

I handed her a napkin to dot her eyes. "Who is Mr. Simpleton?"

"He's the lawyer."

"So this lawyer shows up and convinces you to leave, and at the time, never brings up the topic of the burial in the cemetery."

"He mentioned there was a family plot, not that my husband had to be buried there."

"Very odd, indeed," I said. "Not going to be an easy case to tackle," I paused. "Have they let you go back in the mansion since you were ousted?"

She laughed just then. "Well, we kinda tried to get in tonight earlier." She motioned to the ghost hunters. "Nate and Troy wanted to do a little ghost hunting, but police tape was still over the door."

El bit her knuckle. "Oh, my. So you were at the house tonight."

"Y-Yes, why do you ask?"

I patted her hand. "It seems there was another little accident at the Butler Mansion tonight."

She gasped. "You don't say?"

Nate's eyes were all aglow. "What kind of accident?"

"It seems another man fell to his death from the upstairs window," I said.

"And the maid?" Betty Lou inquired. "Where was she at the time?"

"She just drove by to see if the police tape had been removed," I informed her.

"Likely story. She probably offed him herself."

I smiled kindly. "And for what possible motive, dear?"

"I-I don't know, but she might have killed my husband, too."

"I thought you said a ghost pushed him to his death?" I countered.

"I'm not sure ... it's all so very confusing. I did hear plenty of sounds and saw a few apparitions, too."

El rubbed her hands. "Seems plausible. I-I mean, I believe in ghosts."

I narrowed my eyes at El and turned back to Betty Lou. "It makes for a tough swallow for most folks. You don't hear of many cases like that."

Troy raised his index finger in the air. "Nate and I have seen many things during our ghost investigations."

Nate raised his fist into a claw-like hand. "I had a nasty encounter with a poltergeist, and I was thrown across a room!" His face whitened as he spoke.

Troy tipped his head and visibly shook as if in remembrance. "That was just one case. I have been attacked too, clawed and briefly possessed."

I shook my head; it was getting too deep in here for me. "It's pretty hard to prove things like that. I'm really more of a facts type of girl." I snapped my fingers.

"You're an unbeliever, Aggie. You're just not open to the possibilities most of us are."

"Eleanor, that's not true. It's just how are we gonna prove a ghost pushed a man or now—two, out a window to their death?"

Troy cleared his throat. "If we could get into that mansion, we might be able to get some type of evidence."

"Not sure how," El said. "I heard the locks were changed."

"Right, El, and now with a second body found on the property, I don't see the police tape being removed any time soon."

"I'm not sure about what is happening, but Herman was a real kind soul. I had no deadly intentions toward him," Betty Lou said, frowning. "He was the best catch—I-I mean man I could have married."

El's face became animated. "It would be pretty darn stupid to off the groom the day after the wedding. He was up there in age. He might not have lasted much longer after the wedding night."

"How true you are, El." I glanced down and asked Betty Lou, "Do you know who the Butler Foundation is?"

"No, I just know they seem to be holding all the cards right now," Betty Lou said sadly.

I paused a moment and said, "So, besides Mr. Simpleton, you had no contact with any of the foundation members?"

Her eyes widened. "Not at all. Do you know who they are?"

"Not yet, but I'll be looking into the matter."

"We'll be," El added.

"I'd so appreciate any help you can offer."

She handed me a card with her phone number. "How can I reach you, G.A.S.P.?" I couldn't help but smile every time I said that word—ghosts—gasp, *too funny.*

They handed me their cards and I glanced down at their empty bowls of ice cream, almost seeing a reflection of sorts. I shook my head for such silly thoughts. Now I'm seeing apparitions in empty bowls that I knew were mirroring the light fixtures overhead. Even now, the ceiling fan was moving at quite the clip, shaking the white globe beneath it.

We went back to our seats and lapped up what was left of our ice cream, which at this point was nearly all liquid. Not that I minded. I always liked it that way, just like a melted Frosty from Wendy's fast food chain.

El and I sat in silence and stared at Lake Huron through the etched glass window of Fuzzy's. The waves lapped slowly, and besides an occasional light from a boat coming into dock, there wasn't any other activity. No *Erie Board of Trade* tonight.

As we made our way outside, the sheriff's car pulled in. Obviously, he wouldn't find his bed for quite some time. We locked eyes as he passed.

On the way back to the car, El confessed, "I half expected you to say something to the ole sheriff."

"I was biting my tongue." I smiled. "The widow gave us all the information we needed."

"Or all that she was willing to impart."

"I thought as much, too."

El slapped her knee. "You sure know how to play sympathetic."

"I knew playing bad cop wasn't going to work with her. We didn't leave the best impression with her the first time."

"Her husband's body was just found and she was acting very suspicious."

"What do you make of her story, El?"

"I'm not sure if she's being honest or just wants us to believe she is."

"She's not off the suspect list just yet. We'll be keeping close tabs on the woman and her newfound accomplices."

"Huh?"

"Kinda strange that the pair of ghost hunters just happen to be in town when her husband died, don't you think?"

"There has been a ghost ship spotted, or did you forget?"

"Still, one day her husband dies and the next she's seen in the company of these men."

"Aggie, it could be you're suspicious of everyone." She snorted. "Am I on the suspect list, too?"

"Right at the top, El," I laughed.

I dropped El off and promised to pick her up promptly at twelve. When I arrived back at my trailer, two things jumped out at me: *The devil will see you soon,* was scrawled across my Winnebago in black paint, and both Sophia's car and Martha's station wagon were in my parking spot.

I stared at the letters with mouth agape, fury coursing through my veins. *I'm gonna kill that witch across the way!* When I glanced that way, I saw she had cleared out. *Figures.*

Sophia came in for a hug and whispered in my ear. "Please, you have to help me." She pulled back and rubbed her arms briskly.

I glanced toward Martha's vehicle. "What's up?"

"I was kinda hoping you could let Martha, I mean Mom, stay with you for a while?"

"A while?"

"She doesn't have any money. She spent all she had for the trip here."

I folded my arms across my chest. "Really? I don't see why that is any of my concern." I knew it sounded cold, but really? "I don't mean to sound that way, but I haven't seen her in years. It's not like she had made any effort to reconnect with me before."

Sophia's hand slid to her hips. "And just how do you think I feel, Gramms?"

"I'm sorry, dear. Of course you're right. I can imagine this is really quite a shock."

"You ain't just whistling Dixie, Gramms. I can't put her up at my place." She went to shuffling her feet. "It just wouldn't work out."

I raised a brow. "And you think it will be any better for me?"

She pleaded with me. "Please, Gramms."

"Why is she still in her car?"

"She doesn't think you'll let her stay, that you told her to hightail it down the road."

"I don't remember using those exact words, but what I said was a close second. I'll let her stay. It's not like you're giving me much of a choice."

"I owe you one, Gramms."

Sophia ran to the car. Martha appeared, and within minutes, Sophia hopped into her car and was off like a shot.

"Well, she was certainly in a hurry," I said nervously. "I guess you'll be staying with me, then."

"I hate to put you out, Mom. I'll find a job soon and be out before you know it. If only they allowed tents in the campground."

"You'll be more comfortable here, dear." I patted her hand. "Don't worry, we'll make it work."

"Wow, who did that to your trailer?"

"Some gypsy, although I feared she might be a witch. One day she started ranting 'the devil will see me soon'."

"Wow, that is just freaky." Martha swished her hips in time to a tune from a nearby radio that played a dance tune in the distance.

I opened the door and Duchess dove past me and out the door, again. "Well, I'll be. What on

162

earth has gotten into her lately?" I made my way to the refrigerator and piled out lunch meat and cheese. "Hungry, Martha?"

"Thanks for the offer, but I don't eat meat."

"You a vegan?"

"Not exactly. Do you have any hummus?"

"Humma what?"

"It's a thick paste made from ground chickpeas and sesame with a variety of spices." She laughed. "It's quite tasty on whole grain crackers."

"It sounds nasty."

"You should try it sometime, Mom."

"I'm not sure what I can offer you, then."

"Do you have any fruits and vegetables?"

"Not at the moment, but I had planned to take Eleanor to the farmer's market tomorrow."

She smiled at that. "Sounds great!"

She rummaged through the cabinets and came back with granola bars. She took them to the table and ate them like she hadn't eaten in weeks and it was then that I felt like a complete heel.

"You sure are hungry." I gave her a once over and couldn't help but notice her skinny frame. I offered a Diet Coke, but she shot down the offer, too.

"Diet Coke is bad for you, Mom."

"For someone that is a skinny rack of bones, you sure are awful fussy."

She shrugged. "I was quite a plumper when I was younger or did you forget."

"You were healthy."

"Aw, that's what moms are supposed to say."

"I just never saw you as fat is all," I said with heartfelt honesty.

"After having Sophia, I got even fatter, that's when my husband began to stray."

"Some men don't need a reason to stray." I pulled the sofa sleeper out for Martha and brought her the bedding. "I hope this will be okay. I don't have overnight company." *Not since Andrew left town, that is.*

"T-Thanks, Mom. This is great."

I whirled when I heard a scratching at the door. I opened the door and Duchess ran inside full of pep. She jumped and meowed at Martha.

I said while walking to my bedroom, "You two best get along, I'm heading to bed."

Hissing was followed by loud purrs that I could hear all the way to where I was. Duchess just plays bad cat when really she's just a softy at heart.

I hadn't expected for this unusual turn of events, but maybe this is what I needed—what both Martha and I needed. I'm not getting any younger, and maybe it's time I get to know who Martha really is as an adult, anyway. She needs to know it's no nursing home for this old broad. That's what they say, be nice to your children because they'll be the ones picking out your nursing home. Not that funny of a joke, now that I think about it. I smiled just the same at what kind of havoc El and I could get into.

CHAPTER SIXTEEN

I woke up with fur tickling the inside of my nostrils. I began to hack and cough until Martha ran into the room, her eyes searching me with concern.

"Are you okay?" she inquired.

I nodded. "Yes, just hacking up a hair ball."

"Cats are known to be good for that. I try and stay clear of them, but that cat of yours won't take no for an answer." She smiled.

"I know, but she's quite lovable when you get used to her."

She glanced around, "Hey, does your shower work?"

"I guess. I haven't used it before."

She looked sideways at me. "Wh-Where have you been taking a shower?"

I sat upright. "Campground shower room."

Her face twisted into a sneer. "Yuck. No offense, but you're asking for some kind of fungus doing that."

"Since when is a woman that practically lives in a station wagon so dang fussy?"

She smoothed her hair back. "I know when to be careful, and Mom, you should be extra careful."

"And why is that?"

"Somebody already wrote the devil will see you soon. It may be a warning."

"More like a scare tactic. Believe me, Martha, I know I'm no saint, but the devil wants to see me no more than I do him."

She whirled and said over her shoulder, "I'm gonna scrub up the shower and give it a Girl Scout whirl."

"You were never much of a Girl Scout, dear. Two badges, from what I recollect."

She turned at the bathroom. "I got a cooking badge," she said with pride. "It's not my fault I wasn't good at tying knots, although the other girls sure had me pegged for stupid."

I stood and did my attempt at a stretch, swallowing a groan. "How's that?"

"At camp they told me they were planning to tie me to a tree and let a bear eat me."

"That camp was in Frankenmuth, Michigan. No bears around that area."

She gasped. "Tell that to a ten-year-old!" She shuddered. "I was scared they'd actually do it."

"Trauma at the Girl Scout Camp." I shook my head in disbelief. "I'd have sued if a bear had eaten you."

"What good would that had done if I had been eaten for real?"

"Are you planning to clean the shower or..."

Martha tossed me a look only a daughter could give her mom and nobody else. She rummaged under the sink and after finding the right products, cleaned the shower.

I cooked the remaining bacon and welcomed the aroma that only a meat hater wouldn't enjoy. For some reason that made me smile. Too bad the bleach smell drifted toward me and burrowed up my nostrils from the shower area.

Martha beamed like a child as she appeared and retrieved towels, soap and shampoo. She went to humming in the shower, and I tried to block out the sound of her voice. It was unsettling for me and made me feel sad for allowing my daughter to shut me out for so long. I should have hunted her down and helped her when she desperately needed the help. *If only I had known. Maybe it's not too late to reconnect with her.*

I sure hope that the sheriff doesn't find out that we told Betty Lou the low down on the recent body being discovered at the mansion. As if on cue, there was a knock at my door and I yanked it open, staring down the good sheriff.

"Peterson," I said, letting him inside.

He scratched his head. "Just one question."

"Okay, go ahead." I waited for the blow that

was about to come. Lord knows the good sheriff never brought me good news.

"Did you tell Betty Lou Butler about the body of the handyman at the mansion?"

"I thought he was the gravedigger."

"He was also the handyman."

I bit my lip. "I suppose he'd have to do something besides dig graves. It's not every day a Butler descendant dies, recent events aside."

Peterson narrowed his eyes. "Agnes Barton, are you purposely trying to dodge my question?" From behind clenched teeth, he said, "Did you or did you not tell Betty Lou Butler about the man found dead at the mansion?"

"So he was dead, huh."

"Agnes!"

"Fine. I did, I'm afraid." I smiled weakly. "It's just when the maid told us she had been at the house earlier in the day...I just wanted to know."

He rubbed his head with one hand. "You are not making my job any easier."

"I know and I'm sorry, but—"

"How am I supposed to gauge the woman for a reaction about the handyman's death if she already knew?"

I put my hands up. "I'm sorry is all I can say. I didn't go looking for her. She just happened to be at Fuzzy's and—"

"You just had to butt in."

"Now, Peterson, that's just not fair."

"I was told to speak calmly about the matter with you, but if it happens again, you'll be cooling your heels in jail." He walked toward the door.

"I see. Well, I don't think Trooper Sales will go along with that."

He suddenly whirled and said. "He's the one that sent me here." He grinned. "I guess your granddaughter and you don't have him on quite the string you think you do."

I gasped. "And that means what, exactly?"

"Oh, come on, Aggie. You know what's going on with those two. The whole town knows."

My mind raced and I had half a mind to slap the bejeezus out of him for making me think what I was about Sophia.

"Don't you dare speak badly of my baby," Martha shouted from the doorway. She stood completely naked and Peterson looked about ready to choke as his face reddened.

"Never seen a naked woman before?" I asked.

His eyes shifted to me.

"I'm going now." He raced out the door and ran smack into it as he stumbled out. "Christ Almighty!" He yelled. He jumped into his cruiser and stones peppered my camper as he left.

I raised a fist in the air. "I swear I'm going to sue the county for damages." I whirled to face Martha again who was donning jeans and a purple tee. Wh-What do you think he meant?" I closed my eyes tightly. I didn't want the answer.

"I-I'm not sure, but I think it's possible Trooper Sales and Sophia may be more than just friends."

Stabbing pain struck me in the chest. *No, this can't be happening.* "I can't believe it! He wouldn't do something like that."

Martha patted my hand. "He's a man isn't he?"

"I know, but he's also one hell of a trooper and he wouldn't cross the line like that."

Martha towel dried her hair. "It's not criminal, you know."

"He's a good friend and he should know how I'd feel about this. He just wouldn't do that!" I shouted.

Martha smirked. "Calm down already. You're gonna blow a gasket and I'm not sure if they still make the ones you'd need for replacement."

"How would you know? You haven't been around since Sophia graduated high school."

She winced. I knew I had struck a nerve.

"When you're over your Mother Teresa thing I'll be waiting outside." She ambled down the steps and said over her shoulder, "You did say we're going to the farmer's market today, right?"

I slammed the door shut and wanted to throw something, possibly at Trooper Sales when I caught up to his cagey ass.

CHAPTER SEVENTEEN

I took a shower in my Winnebago, but the water was way too cool and that hadn't helped my mood. All I could think about was wringing Trooper Sales neck first chance I got.

I pulled on white shorts and a pink Victoria's Secret tee. I filled Duchess's food dish and was out the door. I made my way to the Caddy that at this point was more mine than El's. Martha hopped in and rode gangster style. When we arrived at El's house, she was waiting outside with purse in hand.

Martha moved to the back so El could ride up front without a word from either of us.

El jumped in. "I didn't think you'd ever make it here,"

"I almost didn't. Peterson showed up at my door."

"Really? Did he find out about us spilling the beans to the widow?"

"You got that one right." I sighed as I turned onto the highway. "Did you know anything about Trooper Sales and Sophia?"

"Not sure how you didn't, dear, after the day at her place."

"She told us he slept on the couch that day."

"Maybe he did? We shouldn't jump the gun, not that I'd blame the man. Sophia is quite the looker."

"It runs in the family," Martha volunteered.

"I don't want anyone in town talking about my granddaughter."

"Folks are gonna talk. They go jogging together and have even showed up at Hidden Cove. We have seen them there ourselves," El said, patting my hand sympathetically.

My brows drew together. "There could be a lot less jibber-jab in my opinion."

"We'd be straight outta business if that were to happen," El said.

I pulled into the farmers market, which was already packed. This one was held once a year in Tadium. Most of the senior citizens in town were here, and lots of tourists from the looks of the amount of campers parked in the gravel lot.

As we made our way down the pathway of vegetable-laden tables, my mouth watered as I spotted fresh tomatoes, sweet corn, and green beans. Mr. Wilson was sitting beneath a tree fanning himself and Rose Lee Hill waved at us from behind a table. Her fare looked like potpourri just as her sons told me the other day.

From growing marijuana to potpourri. Who knew?

I greeted Wilson. "Are you okay, Mr. Wilson?" I inquired.

"Oh, Aggie, it's good to see you, dear."

When Eleanor whirled near him, she sneered. "Where is the retired school teacher?"

"Oh, sweet Eleanor, you don't have to be jealous. You know you'll always be the one for me."

"Humph." She strode away, making quite the distance between them.

I fanned myself with my purse. "She'll cool off."

"How about you, Aggie? Are you gonna cool off and give that lawyer man a break or do you like them to come begging?"

I tried to act nonchalant. "Andrew is the past. He has a girlfriend or something."

"He doesn't look like she's with him now." He pointed in Andrew's direction. "Might be a good time to make your move."

"Don't be silly, and I have no idea why I'm even having a conversation with you about him." I snapped. I hadn't meant to act like I cared. "Take care, Wilson. Stay here in the shade."

He nodded and sipped from his tea. "Tell Eleanor I'm still in love with her." He winked.

That just made my skin crawl. The thought of

the frail Mr. Wilson and Eleanor together brought back some unsettling memories.

I whirled away and tried my best to avoid Andrew, but I caught sight of him approaching from the corner of my eye. I started picking up zucchini and gave them a careful inspection. I had to do something, anything to not look into his sexy bedroom eyes. It's bad enough I could smell his cologne that about brought me to my knees. I just love a good-smelling man. It's one of my weaknesses right up there with chocolate fudge sundae with toasted coconut.

"Remind you of anything, Aggie?" Andrew taunted me from behind.

I whirled with zucchini in hand and with a straight face, said, "It sure does." I smiled smugly. "I can make this into a killer zucchini bread."

He laughed at that. "That's what I was thinking, too." He cleared his throat. "I'd love to come over sometime for a *piece*."

Just then his phone rang and he stepped away, turning his still gorgeous rear end toward me.

"That's a mighty fine ass if I ever saw one," the woman behind the table said.

"He works out I think," I muttered.

"He can work out on me anytime."

I eyed the woman who was in her fifties. She wore a wicked grin and midriff tee with skimpy shorts.

"I don't think he's available."

"That don't bother me none." She winked.

"Your husband behind you might object." I snickered as the tall, much older man began to holler at her. Not that I thought a marital argument was funny mind you, but she was talking about my Andrew here. *Oh my, I really need to quit thinking like that.* It just burned my bum that he was obviously unavailable, but continued to toss me signals. You just can't go around winking and such if you're dating someone else. At least not in my book.

I made my way toward Eleanor who was examining tomatoes like a CSI agent. "Do you want me to get your magnifying glass, dear?"

"You have to be careful these days. Who knows what kind of varmints might be hiding on these vegetables."

I raised a brow. "Really? Insects, perhaps?"

She giggled. "Oh, Aggie, you don't want me having an infestation like last year do you?"

"It seems like you are already infested with enough varmints already."

Hands went to her hips. "I think not!"

She mentioned her squirrel. "What about Rattail?"

"That's not very nice, Aggie. I just had my hair done yesterday."

I gave her a dead stare. "I know, I wish I could

delete the images from my memory banks." Thinking about the chin wax El had yesterday made me shudder. "You might need to get your hearing tested, dear."

"It's not that, it's just that the doctor has me on some new meds and they aren't quite agreeing with me." She broke wind just then, almost as emphasis.

I waved a hand, clearing the air. "I see. Too much flatulence, then?"

"Yes, and I keep seeing," she glanced over her shoulder to see if anyone is eavesdropping, "well, bugs."

"What in tarnation does the doc have you on?" I gasped. "I have heard of hospice patients seeing things like that, but they are just..." I did my own look around and whispered in El's ear, "over-medicated."

"With good reason."

"I know, but I just wonder who all those drugs are for, the patient or the doctor. It just broke my heart last week to visit Maxine at the County Medical Facility and see her all hopped up on drugs like that."

"Aggie, you know the old dear has dementia. She had the whole place searching for her missing pearl earrings, the ones she was wearing!"

I shook my head. "Poor dear, what is the name of the med you're taking, El?"

Eleanor rifled through her purse and set her pink pistol on the table next to the vegetables, and pulled the medicine bottle out.

The woman behind the counter raised her hands high in the air and screamed. "It's a robbery."

Seniors hobbled away with their walkers, purses clutched to breasts and the men held their frail hands against the pocket that contained their wallets, while the younger folks took off like a shot in the air.

"It's not a robbery," I said. "See, the gun isn't even loaded." So just to prove my point I pulled the trigger. An explosion split the air and seniors toppled to ground, hands pressed against their chests.

"That's just great, Aggie," El said as she took the gun from me and shoved it in her purse. "You just committed a mass murder."

My mouth fell open.. "I did what?" I jerked to face the seniors sprawled out on the ground.

"Yup, it's a mass heart attack."

"That's not funny, El! We need to call 911 or something."

"I already did," a soft voice behind the table said.

"You can stand up, everyone. Nothing to worry about here, j-just a little accident." I whispered to El. "I thought you said the gun wasn't loaded."

"It wasn't, but after the bank robbery I thought it best to load it. Who knows what else might happen."

"Good point, but this is hardly the place to be taking your gun out."

The sirens that roared close by told me that we were once again in a heap of shit. Trooper's swarmed the farmer's market as Sheriff Peterson advanced toward the two of us.

"It's okay, folks. The state of Michigan armed the two of them. Complain to them." He wiped at his nose. He then picked up a tomato and took a bite. "Quite ripe and juicy." And with tomato juice dripping from his chin to his uniform he winked.

Eleanor shuddered, which sent vapor waves of cheap perfume to waft in the air.

"That is the worst smelling perfume yet, El! Where in the heck did you get that?"

Without batting an eyelash, "Walmart, it was on sale."

"It should have been a throw away." I grimaced. "Oh, I feel sick in my stomach now."

Trooper Sales approached. "What happened?" He eyed the woman behind the table who opened her mouth until Sales hushed her with a finger motion.

"El was just looking in her purse and set it on the counter." I shrugged. "Then that woman there started yelling 'It's a robbery'."

"It was all very innocent," El added. "Aggie thought the gun wasn't loaded and cracked off a shot."

"It was all El's fault. She promised to keep it unloaded."

"Agnes Barton, that is a complete fabrication of the truth."

I turned on her. "You know dang well you shouldn't be carrying around a loaded gun."

"We're private investigators and we need one," El huffed.

"And what for?" Peterson said. "You plan to start a crime spree?"

I stepped forward. "You planning to solve the murders in town?"

"They weren't murders, they were accidents!" he bellowed.

My head neared his until we were practically eyeball-to-eyeball. "That's a heap of dung and you know it."

"We are still investigating!" He yelled, his face turning near purple. "If you're gonna play superheroes, you might want to consider Batman. He doesn't carry a gun."

"Batman wouldn't last a day in this town," El said.

"Make up your mind. Were they murdered or did they die accidentally!"

"Are you okay, Peterson? You don't look so good," El cut in.

Peterson's entire face was near blue now, his breath coming in short pants as he fell to the ground.

El wrung her hands. "Oh, Aggie, you done killed the man. We're going up the river for killing the sheriff!" she screamed.

"Oh, damn!" I knelt and started unbuttoning Peterson's shirt exposing his white tee underneath. "Somebody call an ambulance, this man needs CPR." I made a quick assessment and motioned Eleanor into position. She gave Peterson thirty compressions, and then it was my turn. I puckered my lips, almost gagging as my lips met Peterson's and I gave him two breaths. It was then that I remembered he had eaten a tomato! His face was still layered with tomato juice and it was gross. When I lifted my head up and Eleanor commenced with compressions, Peterson's eye lids snapped open and he began to scream. "Get these old bats off me! Help! Somebody, please!"

El and I jumped back to our feet and it was then that I could contain the bile no longer and hurled at El's feet. I swiped at my mouth, but it was too late! When I looked down at my arms the splotching had already begun.

Sales helped Peterson up and into a chair. "These two old bats, as you call them, saved your life."

He shook his head violently like the mere thought was too much for him.

El looked at me oddly. "What's wrong with your face, Aggie? It's swelling up like a big fat balloon."

I nodded and managed to squeak out. "He had tomato juice on his lips."

El ran around in tiny circles. "Somebody call an ambulance quick! She's allergic to tomatoes."

I would have told El how ridiculous she looked, but everything went black.

I heard the sirens in the distance and my body was moving like I was in a boat, which made my stomach ache even more. I just couldn't open my eyes no matter how hard I tried and managed only to concentrate on my breathing lest I die right here and now.

CHAPTER EiGHTEEN

I lazily opened my eyes with El's face near mine, large fake eyelashes framing her blue eyes. "Oh, Aggie's awake!" She jumped up. "Look everyone, she finally opened her eyes."

"Everyone," I mouthed. I turned my head to see a teary-eyed Sophia with Trooper Sales huddled together. Andrew came into the room, took my hand in his, and kissed the back of it while Martha lingered in the distance. She had an expressionless look on her face. I'm not sure if she felt out of place or just wished she were elsewhere. I felt the vast distance between us and it was unsettling. *How could my own daughter not be able to stand in the same room with me ailing as I am and not at least try to comfort me?*

"Are you having a party here or what?" I asked. I eyed the bright sunlight coming through my hospital window that clearly revealed a less than customary decor. Why, the wallpaper border had fish on it while the window covering had God-awful green stripes.

I tried my best to soften my features; Lord only knows what kind of expression I had plastered on it. "What? Mum's the word? I have six months to live?"

"That's not funny," El scolded me with a wag of her finger. "Six minutes." She then belly-laughed and I knew I was going to be okay.

"You're a horrible liar, El."

"And you are just too much. How am I gonna solve this case without you?"

"You mean there still is one?"

"Well, yes. Two people fell from the third floor at the Butler Mansion or did you forget." She bit her finger. "I hope dementia hasn't set in."

"Me, too, because I'm planning to be a handful."

"I wouldn't mind that," Andrew smiled. "I'm sort of used to it."

I sat up with the help of El, and Martha helped me to the bathroom, stepping up at last. "Is your brother, Stuart, here Martha?"

She frowned. "I tried calling, but I couldn't reach him."

"What is it about my children and them not wanting to let me know where they are?"

Martha stared at the wall and then met my eyes. "He works for the government the last I heard."

"Oh, my. Why didn't he tell me?"

"I'm sure he didn't want to worry you, Mom. He'll show up when he's ready."

"I sure hope it's before my funeral."

When I had returned the doctor poked his head in the room. His blond hair framed his handsome face and was a welcome sight. "Aggie, it's good to have you back."

"How long was I gone this time?"

"It's been a few grueling days," Andrew said. "I-I…" He broke eye contact like he wanted to say more.

"I'm sorry to be such a bother," I said. "But I really need to get home before my cat goes psycho."

"She already is that." Andrew showed me his clawed up arm.

"Poor dear was probably scared of you."

"She has been chasing hellhounds all day I'm afraid," Martha added. "It seems Leotyne moved on the opposite side of the campground to get away from you."

"Me? What did I do?"

Eleanor scolded me. "You did set fire to her camper, dear."

"Not on purpose!"

"Still, all she did was put a thorn in your side so why are you so upset?"

"I'm not. It's just that I wanted to be the one that got her expelled from the campground," I huffed. "And now you're saying she's still there."

El laughed. "The campground is big enough for the two of you, just don't go past her site."

"Any more ghost ship sightings?"

"No," El said, disappointed. "But I heard a few folks reported seeing a ghost at Robinson's Manor."

"Now that one I believe since an entire family was murdered there." I shuddered.

"I hope it doesn't hinder their party," El said with a pout.

"Party?"

"Yes," El gushed. "They are doing a charity fundraiser."

"It's a real life Clue game dinner party," Martha said. "I want to be Miss Scarlet."

"Aw, I wanna be her," Eleanor pouted.

Martha looked down her nose at El. "You're too old to be her, maybe Mrs. White."

Eleanor squared her shoulders. "Who you calling old, Marta!"

"Martha," she corrected her.

"How would I know what your name is? Aggie never says a word about you. For all we know you're not even her."

"Eleanor, stop this now. Martha is every bit my daughter."

"Never speak about me, huh?" She made her way toward the door. "I know when I'm not welcome." She opened the door and slipped outside.

"Eleanor Mason, what has gotten into you?"

She wrung her hands together, swaying her body like she was ashamed, but I wasn't buying it a bit. "W-Well s-she started it! I'm not a day over forty."

"Are you talking dog years here, El, because I have known you long enough to know that you're eighty-two."

El's arms folded across her chest and a full on pout lip came out.

I massaged my brow. "Please stop, I'm not feeling well, El. I just woke up from a coma, or did you forget."

"Coma? Seriously, Aggie. I believe you have to be out a whole lot longer than a few days for it to be classified as a coma. Although I heard the brain scans didn't turn up anything."

I narrowed my eyes to slits. "Meaning what?"

"Oh nothing, just that your brain is missing." She clapped her hands smartly. "I think that should be our next case." She pulled up the blankets and looked under the bed. "Nope, it's not under the bed." She tiptoed to the curtains, snatching them back and shook her head. "Not behind the curtains either. I think we have us a caper on our hands."

I smiled behind my hands, not wanting to encourage her.

"I'll check back with you tomorrow," Dr. Thomas said shaking his head, but hightailing it before I started to whining which I did just as soon as he left. "I can't wait until tomorrow."

"Don't even think about asking me to help you this time around," Andrew said. "You need to rest."

"You need to go back to your girlfriend or whoever she is."

With a raised brown, "Are we back to that again?" He shook his head as he made for the door. "Did it ever occur to you that you have it all wrong?"

Before I could say another word, he disappeared.

El discreetly shuffled toward the door.

"Where are you going in such a hurry?"

"He's kinda my ride home, and I was promised dinner. If that woman shows up I'll figure out a way to find out who she is."

Again I opened my mouth and again another person disappeared before I had a chance to protest. Not much else to do but go back to a restless sleep.

CHAPTER NINETEEN

Just like clockwork, I was sprung from the hospital two days later and Sophia took me home.

"So what's new?" I eyed her intently.

Sophia brushed a strand of hair off her arm as she walked me into my camper. When I glanced around — my beautiful trailer was in complete disarray. Drawers had been thrown open, the contents cast across the floor.

"Oh, my." I sunk to a misaligned coach cushion. "Did Martha do this?"

"I'm sure she didn't, Gramms. I-It had to be somebody else" Sophia focused on the mess.

I shifted my eyes to the right. "Are you sure? I mean what do we know about Martha for sure? We haven't seen her in years."

Just then Martha walked in and gasped. "What in the hell happened in here?" She trembled, her face devoid of color.

"I'm not sure. Do you know what happened here?" I asked.

"N-No, but—" She chewed a fingernail. "I-I have s-something to tell you."

Oh, here it comes. I tried to prepare myself.

"I had this dude I was trying to get away from, you see. I had thought I gave him the slip, but now I'm not so sure."

"Dude? Does he have a name?"

"Yes, it's Ernie Lockheart. He's sort of a petty criminal."

I tried to get up, but Sophia stayed me while she called the police.

"How petty are we talking here?"

"Robberies, mostly," She glanced away. "And an occasional bank job."

"He robs banks!" I gasped. "Did he rob the bank in East Tawas?"

"There was a bank robbery in East Tawas?"

"Yes, not long before you showed up in town." I sighed. "Spare me the description though. I doubt that I could even pick him out of a police lineup."

"Why is that, Gramms?"

"Funny thing about when someone puts a gun in your face. You aren't thinking what the perp looks like, you just want to get the hell out of there. Then there was quite the storm that passed us by, and we were holed up in the safe."

"Oh, my. Bill never said that part," Sophia said. "I-I mean you k-know Trooper Sales."

I nodded at her curtly and waved my hand at her. "None of my business, dear." Truth was I didn't want to know.

"Gramms, we're just friends."

"I know all about how the friend thing goes. I have lived a bit, too."

Just then a rap at the door was quickly answered. Perhaps they both wanted the subject dropped.

Trooper Sales came in and took a look around. "Everyone okay?"

"I guess. This isn't the kind of homecoming I imagined."

"Anything missing?"

"I'm sorry, Sales, but I barely had the time to take stock of the place. I have just been victimized again is all." I buried my head in my hands and shook my head. *What next?*

I stumbled outside, moved to tears. *Why does something bad happen everywhere I live?* I wondered to myself.

I turned just as Leotyne strolled back, but this time, her expression was quite somber. "The devil not find you this time, but he'll be back."

My mouth gaped open. "It's a premonition then?"

She walked by without saying another word. Maybe that's why she wanted to move her camping site. *Maybe the fire had a little to do with it.*

Trooper Sales came to me with a police report for me to sign and he left. Martha stopped me from getting up. "Mom, let us clean up the place, just rest there and take it easy." How was I meant to do that; act like my camper wasn't just trashed? I quietly snuck off in my red-hot Mustang before either of them missed me. I don't think the hum of the engine was even noticed over the frantic shrieks inside the camper.

When I arrived at Eleanor's, a blue Impala was parked sideways in the driveway. I raced inside fearing the worse. She wasn't in the house, so I raced to the deck, nearly tripping over discarded clothing. Eleanor was sitting in a chair with her back to me.

"El-Eleanor?" My mind raced, wondering what I had just walked into when Mr. Wilson appeared. He waved. Lucky for me his lower region was blocked by the high-back chair. All that pasty-white wrinkled skin made me want to hurl.

I whirled around, covered my eyes and thought about clawing my eyeballs out for good measure.

I watched from between spread fingers as Mr. Wilson grabbed his clothes and donned them leaving through the open patio door. "Party pooper," he called out.

Eleanor got up; her flip flops flapping across

the deck like flippers. She dressed and walked inside, ignoring me.

"My trailer was ransacked," I said.

That got her attention. "Do tell," she said pouring ice and tea into two frosted glasses, handing me one.

I felt out of breath, so I sat down and took a big gulp, wiping my mouth with the back of my arm.

"That must have been some scene to have rattled you this bad."

Tears filled my eyes, dropping to my lap. "You should have seen it. They went through my belongings like a savage beast and now Martha has admitted her estranged boyfriend might be behind it!" I took another gulp. "She said he robs banks too!" I did breathing exercises to calm myself down before I was in a full on panic attack!

"Okay, so that's two mysterious deaths at the Butler Mansion, a bank robber, and now an estranged boyfriend. This is snowballing real fast and I don't want to be around when the avalanche starts."

"I have no clue why somebody would tear through my camper like that. I haven't even pinned down a suspect yet. Betty Lou Butler is our only viable one at this point."

"Or the maid," El pointed out. "But I'm not sure why either of them would ransack your camper."

"We need to tail Betty Lou, but I'd sure love to check out Robinson's Manor to find out what, if anything, is going on."

El nodded her head. "I'm game."

"Sorry for the interruption."

She shrugged. "Next time I'll leave a note on the door, 'Aggie, stay away'."

"It's just I didn't know what Wilson drove and when I saw the Impala—"

"You kinda went into rescue mode."

I nodded. "I guess." I excused myself and went to try and make some sense of my hair and met El outside and whipped out the door a little too fast because that squirrel Eleanor kept as a pet squawked at me before darting up a tree.

"Damn little rat needs to be exterminated," I said out loud.

"I heard that," Eleanor replied. "He's a bit of a handful. If he had a way over to your camper, he might be the culprit that messed it up."

I laughed. "At this point, I wish that was all it was."

We climbed into the Caddy. El must have driven it home after I was admitted to the hospital. We rumbled up the road and down the long and winding trail through the woods that led to Robinson's Manor.

I gripped the steering wheel. "I still can't believe that this manor turned into a bed and breakfast and stays so packed."

"I hope this ghost story is for real. I'd love to meet a ghost face-to-face."

"Sure you would, El. That's what they all say, until they meet one. I'd rather not, myself. I don't mind staying a skeptic."

"Whatever reality you wanna live in, Aggie, is fine by me."

We cleared the path just as a crow flew overhead. "That can't be good," I said.

When I parked, we walked inside and my archenemy, Mildred, was present in the dining room alongside, Elsie, and *that woman* I had seen Andrew with!

Elsie waved us over and I had no choice but to wander over there. "Hello, Aggie," Elsie said from beneath a wide brimmed blue hat that matched her outfit like always. It would teach me to tell Elsie that she looked good in powder blue. It seemed that's all she wore these days. "I heard you were in the hospital."

Mildred and I were glaring at each other and I never heard the question until Eleanor nudged me in the ribs. "Ow! Yes, I had an allergic reaction to—"

"I heard you saved Sheriff Peterson's life, any truth to that?" Mildred said with a grave voice; her face puckered up like she had just sucked a lemon.

"TH-That day is a bit hazy."

Eleanor puffed up her chest. "We sure did I did chest compressions and Aggie did mouth-to-mouth on ole Peterson." She leaned in. "Even though she knew he had just eaten a tomato which she happens to be allergic to."

"That's pretty dumb if you ask me," Mildred squawked.

"Well nobody did ask you, dear," I said sweetly.

Mildred rose to her feet, but El eased her back to her seat. "Have you ever been in a life or death situation, Mildred?" She paused and when Mildred opened her mouth to speak, El continued. "Have you ever had to make a split-second decision in the heat of the moment? I think not. You just don't think, you have to react and do something real quick like." El had her hand clenched into fists.

"You two are to be commended," the silver haired beauty said. "I'm Evelyn or Evy to my friends."

I stood erect, "Evy what?"

She laughed. "Why, Evy Hart, dear. I thought you already knew that."

Tiny knives stabbed at my heart. Andrew is married. "So are you from Michigan?" I pried. I wanted details.

"Lord no, I live in New York City." She sighed. "And I'm going back just as soon as I talk Andrew into it."

"That's nice. I'm sure you and Andrew will be very happy in New York." Turning to the girls, I said, "I'll see you ladies later. El and I are here on business."

We trounced away, heads held high and ignored the ladies talking. "Why, I never," followed our retreat.

Tears threatened to spill, but I sucked it up. Part of me died, but I knew for certain that Andrew was married and that was that.

"Excuse me," I interrupted a server. "Is there someone I can talk with about the recent ghost sighting here?"

She turned and chatted excitedly and spoke for the moment about what a thrill it was to work at a *real* haunted house. That was until a man with a black suit led us into the study where leather bound books lined the curved bookshelves.

"Wow, this is amazing." I ran my hand across the books in wonder. "A real, old fashioned book to hold in your hand."

"Who would have thought that would happen in this digital age."

"Yes, true. I still like to hold an old fashioned book in my hands."

A well-dressed woman in her forties glided in and shook my hand. "Agnes Barton, it's great to finally meet you. I'm Frances Bowdine. My husband and I own Robinson's Manor."

El smiled widely. "Really? That's one story I'd love to hear. Did you know what this house once was?"

El's eager smile revealed just how gullible she was, or so I thought. "My friend, Eleanor Mason, means the murders that happened here."

"My husband told me all of that, but I never really thought much about it. My husband invested a great deal of money into restoring the old place. Of course, we did get it for a great price." She smoothed the invisible wrinkles in her black skirt. Her ruffled blouse hid a small-framed woman, her black hair swept back into a bun.

"Of course," I added. "I can't see any local buying it, not after the horrific nature of the crimes."

"My husband dealt with plenty of bad press after the cold case was solved by you, Agnes."

"Us," El butted in. "I helped."

Frances laughed nervously. "Well anyway, it turned out that we were even more busy than usual. We had a few ghost hunter shows vying to shoot a show here, but we never felt it was a good idea."

"I don't blame you, dear," I said. "There are a few in town and I'm not at all impressed."

El put up her hand as if whispering a secret. "They call themselves G.A.S.P., as in Ghost Association Special Police."

Frances' eyes widened at that. "I think we would be better off without G.A.S.P."

"I agree, but I heard there was a ghost sighting here. Is that right?" I asked.

"I suppose I can trust you two, right? I mean, it's not going to show up on in the newspaper or internet, is it? We don't play up the fact this house was—"

El stuttered. "S-Scene o-of a horrific murder?"

Frances sunk into a leather chair, massaging her brow. "Well, yes, and if you could, please stop saying that."

"Sorry, dear. El here," I thumbed in her direction, "gets kind of excited, well... about everything."

El nodded in response. "Sorry."

"Go on, dear. You were about to say?"

"We had a few people that have sworn on a Bible that they saw a ghostly figure walking the grounds at night."

"Really? Where were they when they saw this?"

"They claim they have seen them while looking out the window, while others claim they saw it from the rooftop deck."

"That is interesting. It could be wildlife and with the lighting you have outside it might look mighty strange."

"That's what I keep telling everyone!" She rubbed her brow. "We have banned the use of the roof top deck temporarily. We told the guests it's under repair, but the truth is that too many were crowding out there and we were worried some poor soul would fall to their death from up there."

"Good thinking," El said. "There has been a lot of that happening in town. Falling from windows I mean."

I shot El a look to silence her.

"It's not my fault we found two bodies this week, Aggie." She turned to Frances. "She's always trying to shush me up, but I wonder if you ever saw anything yourself, Frances?"

"Of course not! I mean things do go bump in the night, but with a house filled with guests and the age of the manor, it's to be expected."

I nodded. "What about anyone besides you?" I noted her hesitation in answering. "Believe me, you can trust us not to tell a soul."

El shivered. "Oh, Aggie, I wish you wouldn't say it like that! All this talk of ghosts and souls is giving me goosebumps."

Oh I'd give you a bump all right, on the head. "Please continue."

"We had a maid who swore she saw Mrs. Robinson standing at the top of the stairs."

"What do you mean, had?"

"W-Well, it seems she must have quit."

My eyes flashed at that. "She quit?"

"She quit coming to work and that is always a sign that you no longer want to work here."

"Did you try and call her?" I countered.

"Why no, she did a no call and that's grounds for immediate termination." She smiled sweetly.

"Do you have this woman's name? I sure would love to follow up on this story."

Frances walked to the file cabinet and pulled out a stack of papers, going through them. "Hmm, Connie Bristol from East Tawas. I don't see an address, but here is the phone number." She then rattled it off. "Please, don't tell anyone I gave you this information. It's not customary for us to release details about our employees or former ones for that matter to anyone."

"I thank you for your candor and I'm not sure why, but I feel that following up this tip is very important."

"We won't tell a soul," El agreed. She then motioned like she was zipping her lip and throwing away the key.

"Is it true you are having a Clue game fundraiser here?" I inquired.

"Why, yes. It's a dialysis fundraiser. My mother was diabetic and was on dialysis for years before her death. It was just an awful thing to watch her wither down to nothing."

"I'm very sorry to hear that, dear. I know dialysis is very hard and having to lay there for hours can't be easy."

"It's very difficult to witness someone you love to go through that." She then perked up, "I thought a murder mystery fundraiser would be perfect."

"I'd love to take part in it."

"Please do. It's tomorrow night."

"Great. How much, dear? My family wants to attend too."

"It's a hundred dollars, but for your family I'll waive the fee."

Eleanor pointed at her own chest.

"It wouldn't be a party without you, Eleanor, I assume," Frances said laughing. Frances led us out and we parted ways. It was quite pleasant outside with a soft breeze blowing. The abundant garden was loaded with various vegetables. When I saw the tomatoes, I about ran to the car. We made our way back to the Caddy, but when we got there, Evy Hart, was waiting for us.

"Fancy meeting you out here like this, Mrs. Hart," El said. "Won't your friends be waiting for you inside? Unless you didn't notice, we are not that popular with Mildred."

"I know. She's really such a sour puss that I did all I could to sit through lunch."

I nodded and walked past her to open the Caddy door, but she stopped me.

"I think we got off on the wrong foot. Andrew told me so much about you, Agnes, that I just had to meet you."

My eyes narrowed. "Really, and that is why?"

El's eyes went to blinking, and I glared at her, but that only encouraged her. "Yes, why is that?" El chimed.

"I think you misunderstood me," Evy said.

"I think I understand everything perfectly. Somehow you wormed your way into Andrew's heart with your big city ways and store-bought looks."

She backed up a few steps at that. "Store-bought looks? I'll have you know I have not undergone any plastic surgery or had any Botox." Her smile vanished, replaced with a notable frown.

"If you frown like that you're gonna get frown lines," El said.

My temper was red hot, but I tried my best to keep my anger in check. "I didn't mean it the way it sounded, but Andrew left town and promised he would be back soon, and well, he came back to town with you!"

She started laughing. "You're too funny, Aggie, just how Andrew said you were. Silly, I'm not Andrew's wife... I'm his sister!"

CHAPTER TWENTY

I stood there for a total of five minutes, my mouth agape and eyes bulging. Had Evy really said what I thought I heard or was I dreaming? Andrew wasn't married or otherwise entangled with another woman? This was too much to handle standing up so I leaned back on the car.

"Why on earth didn't Andrew say so?" I blurted out.

Evy stood there with hands on hips smiling. "He said that he tried, but you kept cutting him off."

El's belly jumped inside like making popcorn in laughter. "You did, Aggie."

I narrowed my eyes at El. "He could have told me!"

"Men and their stupid pride," Evy added.

"I suppose that I owe him an explanation and you both an apology." I hung my head like an errant child. "I kept seeing him with you while he flirted with me the whole time. It was driving me crazy."

"Not much of a stretch, really." El laughed.

"Look who's talkin' Mrs. Heavyweight Champion of Tadium."

"I haven't had a fight all summer with Dorothy Alton out of town." She frowned. "I almost miss the ole girl or at least her husband."

"She's Eleanor's nemesis," I explained to Evy. "You did tackle Mildred, though."

"I had to. She just knocked you to the ground. I can't have the superhero getting hurt. What would us sidekicks do then?" Turning back to Evy, she said, "As you can well guess, Mildred is Agnes' rival."

"Well, it seems you two get into plenty of trouble. Could you two be a dear and drop me off at Days Inn? It's where I'm staying."

I straightened up again as my hip began to ache. "You're not staying here?"

"Staying at a haunted bed and breakfast isn't the top of my list. Did you two know an entire family was murdered here in 1968?"

El and I nodded our heads in unison and we told her about our hand in solving the cold case to which she shuddered like a baby rabbit facing down a hungry wolf. We piled in the Caddy and Evy was such a dear she didn't even fuss a bit about the ripped interior, compliments of Eleanor's pet squirrel Rattail.

We dropped her off and waved, watching her until she walked inside.

"Sister, huh?" El began. "Hate to tell you that I told you so."

"You just did, dear."

"That man is in love with you."

"Perhaps he is, but that just complicates matters. I'm not so sure how I feel. I mean he makes me feel like a school girl and all, but what if we actually hooked up for keeps, I mean." I cleared my throat. "He doesn't live here, you know. What if he wanted me to move to Detroit?"

"You're kinda putting the cart before the horse here, Aggie. You need to win back the man first."

"Martha is staying with me and my trailer was trashed if you remember."

"Of course, I remember. That just happened today."

"You are eighty-two, after all."

"You're running down the hill pretty fast enough yourself, old girl."

"Not fast enough that I don't have time to have a little fun. Andrew is the only diversion I want from our investigating."

"I suggest you take it slow, Aggie. I'd hate to see you get hurt."

"Too bad you don't have the same sympathy for Mr. Wilson."

"Ahh, he's such an animal. You'd be surprised, Aggie."

"I'd rather not have that mental image in my head, if you don't mind."

"Rocking camper is all I have to say to that. Talk about disturbing."

"Most people think we are disturbed and I'm beginning to wonder if my friendship with Elsie is over now."

"Don't be like that. Things blow over pretty quick. Maybe we should find a man for Mildred," El suggested.

"Who do you hate that much?"

She paused as if in thought. "Sheriff Peterson's dad." She smirked. "Not that I hate him, but he is rather randy at least. Remember when he thought we were hookers?"

"Don't remind me, please." I frowned at her. "Did you forget that he's at the County Medical Facility."

"No he's not. I heard Sheriff Peterson sprung him on a trial basis. He hired an around the clock companion for him, Raul."

"Does Raul have a last name."

"Not that I heard of. He's from Cuba—legally they say."

"Hmm, Hal Peterson who can't keep his willie in his trousers and bat shit crazy Mildred, sound like a match made in Hades and highly unlikely."

"Stranger things have happened."

"I can't see it, sorry."

"We could introduce them."

"Elsie would run us outta town on a rail. I'm

thinking more like being chased by townsfolk carrying pitchforks and torches."

We rolled into my parking space and Martha and Sophia practically flew from the camper. I barely got out of the car before they went to lecturing me.

Martha was panting something fierce. "Where? Why?" Her hands planted on her thighs and she leaned over as if trying to catch her breath.

"Sit down, Martha, before you fall out."

Sophia helped her to the picnic table, her own eyes shooting fire. "Seriously, Gramms, you could have told us you were leaving. You were just released from the hospital today."

"Yes, and with your trailer being ransacked, I thought some goon came and grabbed you," Martha added.

Goon was a word I could do without. "No more goons here in town."

"You're right, Aggie, just a bank robber, possibly a double murderer, ghosts and ghost ships being spotted. It's another day in East Tawas."

"I don't need you to remind me that there seems to be a theme going around here," I exclaimed.

"Yes, ghosts," El said. "It's like the whole town has gone crazy over ghosts."

I rolled my eyes. "It's only going to get worse."

"You got that one right," Martha added. "You

received a call while you were gone and someone reported a ghost was spotted in an oven over at Tim Horton's donut shop."

CHAPTER TWENTY-ONE

Ghost *sightings at Tim Horton's, really?* I can't believe this is happening. I was completely off track with my original case, the death of Herman Butler, but shrugged it off. I'm a go-with-the-flow type of investigator.

I threw up my arms. "Now this is just crazy. Okay, who is going with me?"

All hands shot up and we filed into the Caddy that had room enough for all of us. I raced to the scene of the apparition and when we got there, G.A.S.P. was on scene along with half of East Tawas, it appeared. We wrangled our way inside via the back door. Word was that Tim Horton's kitchen air conditioning was on the blink, so I had heard that they kept the back door open.

The manager's eyes were round and I wondered what he was more shocked about, the ghosts or our sudden appearance.

"What happened?" I questioned the manager.

He rolled his eyes. "Great, Agnes Barton is here. What next, the clown patrol?"

"What's your beef, young man?" Eleanor shouted. "You're lucky to have us here to do a proper investigation."

"That's what they're here for?" He pointed at the ghost hunters.

"Fiddlesticks. I'm wondering who called in the 911 on this one."

"I certainly didn't," he arrogantly stated. "Wherever the two of you turn up, trouble follows."

"What did you say your name was, Mr-Manager-trying-to-hinder-the-investigation?"

"This is not a criminal matter, and I'm not telling you my name."

"Joshua Ferguson," one of the workers said. Her uniform was covered with frosting and flour, but her rosy cheeks and bright smile brightened up the kitchen nicely.

"Don't tell her anything, Anna, or you're fired."

I glanced around the kitchen, which was tidy for the most part, considering how hot it was in here. I felt sorry for any poor soul who did the cleaning. I then narrowed my eyes at the man and thankfully, he shut his trap.

Joshua pulled up his brown trousers a bit at my observation, adjusted his tie to loosen it, and swept a hand over his comb-over to put it back in place. It was so hot back here that the man was visibly sweating with damp patches beneath both arm pits.

Evy started, "If you don't mind, Agnes, I'll wait outside." She laughed. "This heat will ruin my hair." She gave it a careful pat.

"Great idea," Sophia said and followed her back outside.

I nodded, expecting no less from her. *We'll all need a shower after this one.* I turned back to Anna. "Can you tell me what happened?"

"When I opened the oven a-a weird *mist* appeared. I was so scared that I dropped a whole tray of donuts."

I spied the evidence of this scattered on the floor. "There will be some upset deputies in town today," I said with a snicker.

The manager stomped his way out of the kitchen and we were free to observe Nate and Jake from G.A.S.P. with their gadgets in hand. The counter moved and the duo of clowns, including the one with the larger than life hair, jumped up and down like children.

"Did you see that?" Nate exclaimed.

"I certainly did, Jake."

"Who are you?" Nate asked. Static came out of a hand held radio of sorts.

"Show yourself!" Jake demanded.

We waited while the two looked inside the oven. He whirled and moved around the room checking for a cold spot. I think that's what they call it on *Ghost Adventures*.

"Good luck finding a cold spot in this hot kitchen," I whispered to El.

I whirled to Anna again. "Are you sure it wasn't just steam rising out of the oven?"

Anna's eyes shifted to Jake and Nate. "I really wanted to meet the members of G.A.S.P. and maybe get out of work early." She shrugged.

The ghost hunters whirled at that. "You mean you called us out here just to meet us?" Troy said.

"Sorry," she said. "I didn't mean to cause this much ruckus. I promise I won't do it again."

"That is completely cool, but this ghost business is serious stuff for us." Nate winked.

"Thank God," Martha exclaimed. "It's hot as hell in here."

We all walked outside where Anna continued to talk to the G.A.S.P. members, giggling like a school girl, not much of a stretch since she was quite young from the looks of it.

Martha migrated over there as well. "Hey look, El, it's the ghost hunter groupies," I said.

"I see that and your daughter is one of them," El observed.

We walked back to the car and I called out, "Coming, Martha?"

"No. I'll catch up with you later, Mom."

My brow twitched in response to Martha's

hasty retreat and we went back to my camper minus Evy, who walked up the street to her hotel room. When I walked inside, the air conditioning was a welcome relief.

We literally fell on the couches while Sophia excused herself, saying she needed to get ready for her jog tonight with Bill.

"Jogging with Bill again?" I wrinkled my forehead. "Why don't they just give me the skinny and get over it?"

"Because it's none of your business," Eleanor said.

"Who says it's not? She's my granddaughter!"

"*You* is who says."

"Still, I wonder why Sophia won't tell me?"

"Because you'll overreact."

"Damn right I will. Sales needs to find someone his own age and leave her alone."

"It's none of your business, Aggie, just like it's none of our business who you decide to shack up with."

"I'll have you know that I just don't shack up with anybody."

"And Andrew?"

"I'm not sure what I'd call that." I gathered a breath. "It's complicated."

"Welcome to the life of romance and such after the age of sixty."

"You seem to be enjoying the 'and such' part

these days, El."

"Things sure change. It's about companionship more than anything, Aggie, but you just can't let those little opportunities pass you by if one comes knocking on your door, you know?"

"Oh, I know all right, dear. I just hope I haven't burnt all my bridges in that respect."

"Next plan of attack is?" El lounged back, Duchess jumping next to her, meowing a response that we couldn't understand.

"It would be a great day for a swim after sweating like a hog at Tim Horton's," I said.

"That would be a great way to cool off." El sprung out of her chair and dashed outside, returning a minute later with the spare swimsuit from her trunk. Within minutes, the purple floral pattern barely covered her breasts and her plus-sized belly looked more pronounced. When I put my suit on, I covered it with a sarong. I just didn't have the devil-may-care attitude about my body that El had. I rather envied her for that. I carried a paunch around my lower belly like most women who had children. My breasts were spared from the downward motion at this point, so I reveled in that.

We grabbed a few towels and made our way toward the beach, passing the gypsy Leotyne who waved at us this time. "She certainly is playing hot and cold," I told Eleanor.

"Yup, maybe distance is all you two ever needed. Next time you decide to start a fire, warn me ahead of time so I can bring marshmallows."

"You are on fire already."

"I don't think so, Aggie. You don't see me mooning over a man."

"I'm not mooning over him, but I'm just not sure how and why I will run into him again."

As we cleared the tree line, Andrew and Evy were on the beach seated in lounge chairs.

Evy waved us over. "I was telling Andrew about our little adventure today."

"What part was that, dear?" I asked.

She winked. "Well, the ghost hunt at Tim Horton's donut shop, of course."

I laughed nervously. "Yes, that was a real waste of time."

"That's not true. Martha might have found a social connection to keep her outta of your hair," El said.

"Great, more rumors to deal with."

"What other rumors could there be?" Andrew asked.

"I'm not at liberty to say at this time."

"More of the same, I see. You haven't changed a bit." He winked.

"Yes, I have. I'm just more guarded than I once was." I needed to stop this conversation before it got out of hand. I had no intentions for it to turn into a disagreement. "We're gonna take a dip."

El and I walked toward Lake Huron where I shucked my sarong, receiving a wolf-whistle from Andrew who looked like sex on a stick in his speedo. *Speedos should be banned—and in front of his sister, no less.*

My dentures chattered. "Damn, it's c-cold in here."

"Quit being a baby, dear. Just keep wading in deeper."

Small pieces of driftwood and minnows moved by our feet until we were in waist deep. When it was deep enough to swim, El and I splashed each other and enjoyed just being friends and not crime solvers, constantly on the move until screams pierced the air.

"What's going on?" I screamed.

"Something slimy over there touched my leg!" a woman shouted, pointing out an area twenty feet from where we were.

I waded over there to investigate and noticed a dark shadow below the surface. And when I gingerly touched it, I screamed.

"What is it, Aggie?" El asked giggling. "It's probably driftwood."

"I-I d-don't think driftwood has fingers!"

"What?" El waded to where I stood. Sure enough, dark hair fanned out from a body just beneath surface. El screamed and made her way

220

toward the beach.

Andrew swam out there and I treaded water until he reached me. The body bobbed against us, layered in seaweed, perhaps the reason it hadn't floated to Canada.

A horrified expression came over my face. "What should we do, Andrew?"

"Someone call 911," Andrew shouted as a crowd had begun to gather. He then turned to me. "We should stay with the body so it doesn't float off."

"W-We c-could pull it to shore," I suggested, to which we tried giving it a tug, but it was so tangled in driftwood and seaweed that it wouldn't move. It was then that I noticed the maid uniform. Although scared half out of my wits, I searched for something, anything that would identify this body as that of the maid from Robinson's Manor, the one who never showed up to work, and was potentially missing.

Andrew's eyes widened. "Maybe we'd better leave it to the sheriff's department," he said.

Tears welled up and fell.

I continued to feel my way along the body, working under the seaweed until my fingers brushed against a circular, hard object. I jerked it out and clasped it tightly in my hand. "Got it!"

"What in tarnation are you doing, woman?"

"I think I know who this might be."

"Who?"

"The missing maid from Robinson's Manor."

"You're losing me."

"Oh, Andrew, I'll explain it when the sheriff gets here." *No sense in explaining it twice is my thinking.*

It was getting darker now, and even the orange and pink sky wasn't soothing me like it usually did. I just wanted the sheriff to get here fast.

Sirens split the air as Sheriff Peterson and the state police were on scene, not a one of them wearing wetsuits. They just carried a metal basket into the water and took over while we waded to shore.

"Please, don't be nasty to me for once, Peterson," I cried as I finally made it to shore and sunk to the sand. Eleanor quickly covered my trembling body with a towel and Andrew took her place trying his best to warm me by rubbing my arms vigorously.

Peterson waded into the lake, barking orders. I couldn't see anything from my vantage point. The sheriff's department had their own watercraft, but the water wasn't deep in the area they were concentrating on.

I shook my head. "This is just eerie."

"Aggie, this is Lake Huron, not Lake Erie," Eleanor said.

I glared at her. "Is that your way to cheer me up?"

"It's the best I could do. So what does it feel like to have touched a real dead body?"

"It's overrated."

"How did you even see it out there?" Andrew asked, now rubbing my shoulders.

"I didn't. A woman screamed and I went to check it out." I trembled. "There was a shadow on the surface and —"

"Floater," El added. "It's not like we were fishing for bodies, Andrew," El spat. "They better hurry. It's getting mighty dark."

"How right you are, El," I said.

The sheriff's department began moving toward shore carrying the basket, which was quickly covered with a tarp of some sort.

Eleanor frowned. "Aww, I wanted to see the body."

"El, that is just awful. I can't imagine it would look so good if it was in the water for any length of time."

"You have that right, ladies," Trooper Sales said as he joined us.

He was dressed in gray jogging attire, his sneakers with glow-in the dark stripes.

"I hope Sophia isn't here."

"No, she went home when this was called in."

"Who found the body?" Peterson asked as they carried the body past us.

I bent my head.

"Thought as much. Come along, Agnes. We can question you back at your camper. Too many ears around here." He coughed. "The crime lab will be here soon and will be taking over here."

"Agreed," I said.

We walked back to my camper and positioned ourselves on the picnic table while Peterson sat across from me. He went through the standard questions like my name, age, and address. Then he asked, "So how did you find the body?"

"We just came back from Tim Horton's—"

"Somebody claimed a ghost was in the oven, if you can believe that," El said.

I glared at El. "We decided to take a dip in the lake to cool off."

"And then?"

"We just waded out and were having fun until a woman screamed. I went to check it out and it was a solid, slimy object. I thought at first it might be a dead fish or something."

El went and fetched us ice tea, presenting us each with a tall glass.

Peterson took a drink. "Thanks."

My hands shook as I gulped down the tea. "I-I reached down and felt what I was sure was a hand and it was, but it was getting dark and I thought I better keep ahold of it until you showed up."

"Good move. It might have floated off and washed ashore somewhere else."

"I'd hate to find a floater," El said, wiping her mouth daintily with a napkin.

"Andrew came out and held the body in place, and then you showed up."

Peterson wrote in his notebook while the bug zapper sizzled insects in the background.

I leaned forward. "The body must have been a woman with the length of the hair. Isn't that right, Peterson?"

"You tell me," he said.

"I got a tip at Robinson's manor earlier that I planned to follow up with."

His eyes were glued to mine. "Like what?"

"I went to Robinson's Manor the other day and the owner, Frances Bowdine, mentioned that a maid, Connie Bristol—"

El slapped her knees. "She had reported that she saw a ghost, if you can believe that."

I continued ignoring El's constant interruptions. "The owner said that Connie never showed up for work the next day. I just felt it was important to try and find the woman."

"Go on," Peterson said.

"I hate finding the body of someone I'm looking for."

"Why, Aggie?" Andrew asked.

"When I find a body that happens to be a person I was planning to question, it leaves the sheriff here thinking I'm responsible."

"I doubt that, sweetheart. You don't go around killing people."

"I know." I put the nametag on the table and slid it toward Peterson. "But I removed this from the body."

"You what?" Andrew said. "Why didn't you say anything?"

"I wanted to wait and tell Peterson first."

"That's your smartest move all year," Peterson said. "But I thought you were investigating the Herman Butler case?" Peterson scratched his shoulder.

"We were, but I thought there may be a connection between the cases.

"What I see is this, Agnes. The whole town is going ghost nuts since those ghost hunters showed up." Peterson stood up. "You have no clue how many sightings that are being called into dispatch." He paused, "Darn reality shows will ruin this country."

"I just thought the ghost angle between Mr. Butler and now Connie might mean something."

Peterson scratched he neck. "How?"

"We were told that Connie saw a ghost at Robinson's Manor."

"Thanks for helping us ID the body, Agnes. If you find out anything else, please share it right away," he said, completely blowing off the ghost theory. "We'll be in touch if we need any more information."

"And the case about the dead handyman? How is that going?"

"The maid was shopping at Walmart before she discovered the body. Her image was captured on camera." Peterson cleared his throat. "And the case is still under investigation."

I nodded as he walked away. "That sounds hopeful."

"The investigation or Peterson's attitude?" El asked.

"Both, I guess."

"Well, you have to admit that Peterson has treated you much better than he did on our last case." She giggled. "He hasn't arrested us yet."

I glared at her. "Don't jinx us!"

"You did save his life."

"And I never even got so much as a thank you!" I replied.

"Stupid male pride," El said. "Isn't that what Evy calls it?"

Andrew interrupted us. "Hey, wait a minute you two. Now you're siding with my sister?"

"Now you tell me that she is your sister."

"You never gave me a chance, Aggie. It was burning me in the worst way."

"What's that?"

"That you'd think I'd just run off and hook up with a woman so quick after what we shared."

"Maybe I should leave," El suggested.

"No," Andrew and I chimed. "Besides, my car is at your place and you shouldn't be driving home in the dark," I said.

"She shouldn't be driving period." He smiled.

We drove El home and I retrieved my Mustang. Andrew and I then headed back to the camper.

When I walked toward the camper, I turned to look hesitantly at Andrew as my brow furrowed. "I suppose you're leaving now?"

"I should really check on Evy, what with dead bodies showing up all across town. We left her at the beach, remember?"

Evy waved from across the way, standing next to a roaring campfire. "You two kids have fun now, I found some people I know. I'll be fine."

We walked inside and Duchess did her classic hiss at Andrew and pawed at his leg.

"That cat still doesn't like me."

"She's just mad that you were gone so long."

Andrew backed me to the counter, his mouth moving in, his body making an unexpected contact with me I hadn't seen coming. "Wh-What are you doing, mister?"

"This." His lips captured mine and I was lost in the kiss. *I can't let this happen,* my mind screamed, but my body spoke otherwise. I finally gave in when my head started spinning, his cologne overwhelming my senses. We ran back to the queen-sized bed, our clothing in a pile on the floor within minutes. We reconnected in the way only lovers could, and I lost myself in the moment.

CHAPTER TWENTY-TWO

I woke up, my limbs entwined around Andrew who was breathing evenly enough to make me believe he was still quite asleep. My mind raced. *So much for holding myself back.* I just hadn't wanted this to happen yet. I'm seventy-two and people our age just couldn't do things like this. I don't just want Andrew in my bed. I wanted his heart and thus far he hadn't said the L-word.

Pans clanged in the other room and I knew coffee was brewing from the fragrance drifting from the kitchen. I bolted upright. Martha had to be home because I'm dang sure that Duchess hadn't learned to make coffee.

"Wh-What?" Andrew tried snuggling me back to him.

"Would you stop it," I whispered. "My daughter is home."

"Daughter?"

"Yes, my daughter showed up recently and she's staying here for the time being," I informed him.

"So, why are you acting like this, Agnes?"

"Because it's weird and this is why I didn't want you staying."

He leaned on an elbow. "Really? You could have fooled me. I think I have claw marks on my back."

"Stop it," I whispered. "She'll hear."

"She's not a child, Aggie. I'm sure she understands that her mother needs a little lovin'."

"Stop it, would you? I'm not comfortable about this situation."

I threw on my robe and went out into the kitchen. Martha was busying herself reading the newspaper and laughing out loud.

I poured myself a cup of coffee as Andrew joined me, clothed, thankfully. I then poured him one and we sat at the table. "What's so funny?" I asked Martha.

She looked up. "Besides the two of you?"

I felt sick to my stomach and cleared my throat. "I'm not sure I know what you mean."

"Next time you hook up leave a bra or something on the door so I'll know."

My face began to burn and I didn't need to look in a mirror to know I was blushing. "I-I...," is all I could choke out.

"I thought poor Duchess had her tail caught in the door with the way it sounded."

My eyes widened at that and Andrew laughed.

"Great comparison, Martha. I'm Andrew by the way."

"Are you planning to stick around or should I go get a shotgun right now?" Martha asked.

He winked. "I'm sticking around. Don't worry."

I stirred creamer into my coffee. "You're not letting me off the hook here, are you?"

"Nope, but you might want to check out the newspaper. You and Eleanor made the front page."

I grabbed the newspaper with a white-knuckled grip. There was a picture of El and me drenched to the gills the day of the fire at Leotyne's campsite. "Oh, great. I'm going to be the joke of East Tawas."

"I think you are already, sweetheart. I'll be leaving, ladies. I have a court date today." He kissed the top of my head and said on his way out the door, "Try to stay out of trouble."

I was so distracted by what the newspaper said that I barely heard him. "I'm never going to live this one down."

"Sure you will, Mom. So, it looks like both of us got a hook up last night."

"Please, spare me the details."

"Nate is so sweet."

I raised a brow. "Isn't he a little young for you?"

"I like 'em young." She made a claw out of her hand. "I'm a real cougar, grrr."

"I told you I didn't want to know."

"You need to lighten up, Mom."

"So everyone tells me."

"You should listen if it's a consensus."

I rolled my eyes and gulped the rest of my coffee, took a shower, and returned dressed in green crop pants, button up jungle print top and sneakers. "Do you want to go the Clue game fundraiser tonight?"

Martha's eyes lit up. "I sure do. What are your other plans for the day?"

"I want to check out the Butler family cemetery."

"Do you mind if I tag along? That sounds like fun."

I shrugged. "Why not, if you promise not to tell El that Andrew spent the night." She did a motion of zipping her lips.

I waited while Martha threw on a pair of denim shorts that were a tad too short for a woman her age and a scoop-neck, aqua shirt. She also opted for sneakers.

I drove to Eleanor's and when we arrived, Mr. Wilson was walking to his car and from the looks of it, a smile was plastered to his face. I had never seen the man move that well before.

He waved as he backed up into the trash cans

and tore away. "He drives just like Eleanor," I observed.

"Really? So Eleanor doesn't drive that well?"

"Haven't you noticed all the dents on her Caddy? How else you think they got there?"

"I thought she bought it that way."

"I assure you that the car was dent-free when I bought it for her."

"You bought her the car? That was sure nice of you."

When we walked inside, Eleanor was in her underwear whistling along to Hank Williams. I waved at her to get her attention and she beamed. "Hello, girls," she said. "Great day to be alive isn't it?"

"I suppose, but our pictures are on the front pages of the *Tadium Press*."

"I heard about that. I've had a few calls asking for a full interview. It seems like we're getting more famous."

Martha lips curved into a smile. "Or infamous."

"I like your style, Martha." Eleanor left the room and returned dressed in purple Capri pants and matching dragonfly shirt.

"Don't forget to wear sneakers. We're going to the Butler's cemetery today."

"In that case, I better bring along my rosary beads." To which she left the room and returned with the black beads clasped in her hands.

"Since when are you Catholic?"

"Never you mind, Aggie." She turned to Martha. "She always has to have the last word."

"And that coming from Little Miss Butt-In-Ski."

Her arms folded across her chest. "Meaning what, exactly?"

"That you kept butting in when Peterson was trying to question me last night."

She stuck her tongue out at me. "Why does it have to revolve around you all the time?"

"You didn't find the body."

Our faces moved closer to each other. "Neither did you, another woman on the beach did."

Martha separated the two of us. "Ladies, please. We are never going to get anywhere if you two don't behave. You're a team, a damn good one from the sounds of it, so cut it out already."

I gasped. "You're right. I'm sorry, El."

El wiped at an invisible tear. "Me too, Aggie." She then wrapped her arms around me, giving me a huge bear hug.

"I-I can't breathe," I choked out.

She released me and the three of us went outside. Eleanor's eyes widened at the contents of her trash cans that was spilt on the ground. "What is the meaning of this," she scoffed.

I laughed. "Blame your Mr. Wilson. I must say I haven't seen the man move with such ease before."

Eleanor beamed at that. "I know, right? He told me that coming over here is better than physical therapy."

"You mean you and Mr. Wilson are doing the freaky-deaky too?"

El looked at me curiously. "Too?"

I glared at Martha. "She means she shacked up with one of the G.A.S.P. fellows. Nate, I believe."

Eleanor snickered. "Did he make you gasp, Martha?"

"He sure did. I reckon I made him gasp more, though."

"Enough with the gasping already," I said, wiping the sweat that had gathered at my brow. The last thing I needed was for her to find out about Andrew just yet. I wasn't ready for Eleanor to find out that he spent the night.

We left for the Butler Mansion and brought Martha up to speed on the case including the Butler Foundation. I then parked alongside the highway. There wasn't a driveway; only a stepping stone pathway led up the hill where the cemetery was located. We waited until all the cars had gone by before we all got out.

"Why are we parking here?" El asked.

"Do you see a road leading to the cemetery?"

"Well, no."

"Okay then." I nodded. "Plus, I don't want anyone to know we are checking out the cemetery is why."

Martha scanned the wooded area ahead. "Why is that, Mom?"

"Are you two coming or are we gonna debate the subject all day?"

"Lead the way, fearless leader," El said.

There was a huge patch of mowed grass with a sign that displayed the name, Butler's Cemetery. It was a plain white sign placed there a few years back to mark the area so people could visit it without going directly to the mansion a hundred yards to the left.

"Oh, phooey," El said as she pointed to the locked fence. "I guess this is a private cemetery." She strutted toward the car.

Martha stopped her with, "Not so fast. I got this."

Eleanor dodged forward and we both watched as Martha pulled a long, metal object from her bra. She then walked to the lock and worked her tool until it snapped open. "Ready, ladies," she said.

I stared up and into a camera. "Shit!"

"Why are you worried, Aggie? The mansion is on lockdown, remember?" El reminded me.

As we entered the pathway, we were practically attacked by dragonflies and sweat bees. "This can't be a good sign," El screeched as we swatted at the bugs. The musty dampness of the cemetery messed with my sinuses and I sneezed.

"We're in the woods. What were you expecting?" I said wide-eyed.

Martha was trembling. "I'm scared. There is something here. I can feel it."

"Don't be silly, it's just a cemetery. Please relax, girls."

El's teeth were chattering. "I-I can't." Her eyes widened as she looked around.

We made it to the first set of tombstones; it was a series of three large stones that were in disrepair. The middle one was carved with the word 'Mother' and the one to the left read 'Daughter', but the one to the right had collapsed.

"Hmm, you can't read that one at all," I pointed it out. "And no dates on any of them."

El's teeth chattered. "I-It's probably the original ones. M-Most likely from the 1800s, around the time when the house was built," she said,

"Not that I have been near a computer in quite awhile, but surely there has to be some information about the Butler Cemetery online," Martha said.

"It's so old there is no information about it online," I said.

El shook her finger at me. "I know, but Aggie, you don't even own a computer."

"I'm so behind the times." I shrugged. "I used the library computer."

"You two need to get with the times if you have an investigator business going."

I rolled my eyes. "That, from a woman who lived in South America for years at a time."

"I needed to throw myself into a noble cause after my divorce."

"And what cause was what? Forgetting you had a daughter and a mother? You could have come to live with me."

"Oh, Mother, really? That is so fifties. Besides we weren't on the best of terms at the time."

"And I suppose that is my fault, right?"

"It's both of ours, I suppose, but how was I going to tell you that my marriage was a train wreck?"

"I'm your mother. You could have told me anything."

"I didn't live in the same town as you, Mom, and I guess I did withdraw myself from not just you but Sophia."

"Would you two stop it?" El insisted. "It's not about what you could have or should have done. It's time for new beginnings."

"You're right, Eleanor. I'm sorry, Martha."

"Ditto. So why are we here again?"

"I wanted to poke around and see if anything looks out of place is all."

Eleanor walked a few paces away. "You mean like a grave that has already been dug."

"Well, they are arguing in court about burying Herman Butler here. I expect that they had already dug the grave in anticipation of doing so."

"Maybe you should step over here and look then."

I had no clue what El meant by that until I reached where she stood and my mouth flew open. My hand trembled as I covered my mouth in shock. There were two grave markers engraved with the names Herman and Betty Lou Butler, both of the graves dug. "Seems like Betty Lou has just moved from suspect to a potential victim," I gulped.

El took out her cell phone and snapped a picture. "I have to agree with you there, Aggie, but how on earth do you explain that to her?"

"I'm not so sure I'd want to know," Martha said. "Of course, if my grave was already dug, I'd be hightailing out of town in a hurry."

We then searched through the rest of the cemetery that included lumber shaped stones, many of which were dated in the 1800s. I read another set of stones, "Letterman ... I thought this was the Butler descendants."

"They might be a Butler," El said. "What with marriages and all. Like Betty Lou."

"Has anyone besides me noticed that most of the Butlers died in pairs, husband and wife?" Martha said.

I stared at the stones and then said, "Either the Butlers are cursed or they are unlucky as hell."

A brisk breeze blew and a tree limb crashed to the ground and we bolted toward the car.

"True, it's another thing to check out. I would love to question the maid again, but I'm unsure if I should ask her about the graves."

"She might be behind it," Martha added. "Can we leave now? Those empty graves make me nervous."

"I second that," El chimed.

We made our way back to the car and tore off the grass in our hasty retreat. I raced back to Tawas and we stopped at Kentucky Fried Chicken.

As we walked toward the counter, the young man standing behind it was none other than Sheriff Peterson's nephew, Clint Peterson. A wicked smile curved on El's face at the recognition, and I almost pitied the young man who had parked in the handicapped parking spot El and I desperately needed a few days ago at the sheriff's department.

Clint's hair was slicked back and I wondered if it had anything to do with fryer oil.

"Maybe we should go somewhere else to eat," I suggested.

"No way, José." El tapped the register to get Clint's attention.

"Are you ready to order, Ma'am."

"Hhmph, Ma'am? Do I look old or something? Is that what you're saying?" She looked around as if certain he was talking about someone else.

"You are kinda old," Clint sneered, then rolled his eyes in a show of recognition.

"You're asking to get yourself slapped. First you park in handicapped spaces and next you have the audacity to call me old." El stomped her foot in mock-outrage.

"Just order, there is a line forming," I whispered.

"Yes, and everyone can hear you," Martha added.

El leaned forward and gripped the cash register. "I'd like an eight piece meal with three pops."

"You mean sodas?"

"Are you deaf boy, or do you live out of state? Here in Michigan we call it pop and I want Pepsi's."

His eyes narrowed. "Why didn't you say that to begin with?"

"Why didn't you ask? Duh?" She smiled as he shifted under her inspection.

"Would you like a ten piece meal for three dollars more?"

"Did I ask for a ten piece meal?" She looked around the room. "Anyone hear me ask for a ten piece meal?"

Nobody dared to utter a word.

"I'm just trying to do what my boss tells me to."

He looked over his shoulder, and sure enough, his boss was watching the situation unfold from a distance.

"Just give me my meal and make it snappy would you? I'm hungry."

Clint's eyes narrowed. "Whatever the customer wants." He went off and literally threw the chicken in the bucket, slammed potatoes into containers, most of which dangled off the sides. He grabbed the coleslaw and three Pepsi's and sat them precariously on the tray, shoving the plates in between the cups.

"Did you ask what sides I wanted? I don't think so. I hate coleslaw and those potatoes look a mess. I want new potatoes in the containers like it's supposed to be, and you forgot my biscuits."

"Do what she says, Clint," the manager ordered him. "The customer is always right."

"Whoever came up with that policy never had to wait on one!" Clint shouted. "And I'm not giving this old bat a thing but this." He flipped us off and dropped his pants, mooning us.

Gasps filled the air as we ambled outside, yet again without any food. "Eleanor, what on earth possessed you to do that?"

"He had it coming after parking in our handicapped spot."

"You two don't look handicapped to me," Martha pointed out. "And who owns a parking spot?"

"I know, but I have no problem using my cardboard sign if I'm feeling tired. Plus, I do have an official one from the doctor, I'll have you know."

"You probably just got that poor boy fired and his boss is gonna call Peterson. I hope you know that." I opened the door and swung behind the wheel.

"Since when do you care what Peterson has to say?" Eleanor asked as she slid into the passenger seat.

"He's just a kid, Eleanor. You're gonna have him hating every senior citizen he meets."

"He probably already does."

"You don't know that. Plenty of nice and kind younger folks around. Who do you think you are, anyway?"

She twisted the ring on her finger. "You wouldn't understand because everyone loves Agnes Barton and just laughs at me, 'Oh there goes crazy old Eleanor again', they say." Tears welled to the surface and she took a tissue out and dabbed at them. "I didn't mean to be like that, but I just couldn't shut it off once I started."

"I know. You're incorrigible, but we need to make amends somehow."

"Like what?"

"Oh, gosh, I don't know. Perhaps help him raise the funds for his parking violation."

"Seriously? I think that is going too far now, Agnes. How can we do that?"

"There has to be some kind of fundraiser we could do that people would be happy to contribute toward."

"The bake sale thing didn't go very well. Maybe we should just sell flowers on US 23."

"Now that is just crazy talk, Eleanor. Be serious."

"We could get him a job at the campground," Martha suggested.

"No, that won't work. He's related to the sheriff and that won't do. The county had some lawsuits some years back and they have to watch it."

"Robinson's Manor might need some help. I should call the owner." I picked up my cell phone and did just that. I smiled when I hung up. "Frances said they need another grounds keeper and would be happy to hire the boy."

We arrived at the sheriff's department and were led inside Peterson's office. His red-eyed nephew was there and I felt even worse than before.

"Peterson." I nodded. "Eleanor has something to say to Clint here."

Peterson, fingers entwined, just sat there with a smile on his face. Files were spread across his desk and I tried a quick look, but with a snap of a wrist, he concealed them from view. *Figures.*

I nudged El forward.

Her eyes shifted as did her feet. "W-Well I'm awful sorry to have caused you any trouble and didn't mean to get you into trouble at work."

"I think we all know I was fired."

"Of course. We made some calls and... well, Aggie did, and we found you another job."

"Not at another fast food joint, I hope."

"Nope. Robinson's Manor actually, as a grounds keeper."

A grin split across Clint's face. "Really? That sounds great. I love to be outside."

"That will be hard work Clint," Peterson said. "Thanks, ladies. I'm glad to know I didn't have to hunt you two down."

I backed away. "Don't look at me. It was all El's doing. She just can't keep her trap shut sometimes."

El's face twisted into a sneer but before she could say a word, Peterson said it for her. "I think you both have issues in that department." And then looking at Clint, "You better get over to Robinson's Manor before the owner changes her mind. I'm assuming Frances was the one offering the position. I believe her husband is presently out of town."

Clint left with lightning speed, either afraid not to do his uncle's bidding or eager to begin his job.

"Robinson's Manor is having a great fundraiser there tonight. A Clue game fundraiser for dialysis," I said.

"Yes, I know. She plans to buy a van to transport patients to dialysis, a great cause since most from our area travel quite a distance for treatment," Peterson said.

"That's for sure. We were asked to be there tonight as guests. She's waiving the fee for us."

Peterson ginned. "Murder mystery, right up your alley."

"It should be fun." I then frowned. "Was the body ID'ed as Connie Bristol?"

"Yes, and the coroner is doing an autopsy."

"I hope we can figure out who killed her."

"That's if it was a homicide. We'll have to wait for the coroner's report before that can be established."

"What bull," I said. "And that will take how long?"

"A few weeks."

El patted my hand. "We need to be patient, Aggie."

"Thanks, Peterson. We'll be in touch," to which he noticeably frowned.

Chapter Twenty-Three

I emerged from the bedroom wearing a black evening gown with silver slippers for the Clue fundraiser, earning a whistle from Eleanor. I patted my liberally sprayed hair that I had gotten done in haste on the way home. El also had hers done and the grey pantsuit she wore hugged her curves like a loose-fitting glove. "Wow, El. You're gonna send Mr. Wilson to the emergency room tonight."

She blushed and then said, "Do you really think so? I'd hate to resort to online dating if he kicked the bucket."

Martha on the other hand wore a jungle print catsuit! She had the body to do it too, but I knew I'd be embarrassed to call her my daughter. Sophia had declined my invitation. "Martha, really? Are you planning to pole dance tonight?"

"You betcha!" She moved her hips suggestively.

I threw my hands up in frustration. "You look like a hooker."

"And you look like an old bird."

I gasped but El broke through my thoughts. "Come on, ladies. Don't spoil our night out."

I was lost in my own little world with thoughts of the recent case. *So the maid was on camera at Walmart at the time of the handyman's death*, I mused. *Yet Betty Lou and the members of G.A.S.P. were at the Butler Mansion earlier, but that doesn't mean that they were responsible. Yet that doesn't make them innocent either*. I was torn from my thoughts when I heard a vehicle tear into my drive.

Andrew arrived with his LX, dressed to the nines in a black tuxedo. He strode to the door with a bouquet of red roses, which he presented to me like in one of those old movies. I blushed, feeling quite embarrassed by the whole thing.

I put them in water, threatening Duchess with bodily harm if she dared to knock them to the floor like she did every other time I had flowers in the house. She rolled on her back in response.

We left with Eleanor riding up front. She just needed a tad more room than I did. Andrew had raised a brow at Martha's appearance, but like the gem he is, he never said a word.

When we arrived at Robinson's Manor they had valet parking. "Frances really has gone all out," I said as we left the LX.

"She's like that," El said.

"Evy isn't coming tonight?" I asked.

Andrew grinned. "She's coming with Elsie."

I frowned.

"I don't have any idea why you care what she thinks. She thinks she's some kinda social icon around here," El said.

I knew she was right, but we had some great times. We all gathered inside and I noticed Betty Lou Butler was dressed in a shimmering green body-hugging gown. We took our places at the table next to hers, and I half wanted to warn her about the open grave with her name on it, but I didn't. I mean, how do you just up and say that kind of thing?

Elsie and crew were seated nearby, too. Mildred was smiling next to goofy-looking Hal Peterson, Sheriff Peterson's dad. When I turned to look at El she shrugged. "How did you pull that off eh, El?"

"Well, I just pointed Hal in the right direction and he asked Mildred for a date. From the looks of it they're hitting it off."

"Good job, El."

"See, there is somebody for everyone," Andrew smiled as Mr. Wilson joined us, sitting next to Eleanor who positively beamed.

"Well, well, Andrew, you're full of surprises," Mr. Wilson said.

"I can be. Wilson was lost without Eleanor," he whispered in my ear as the first course was served.

"I have no idea what this is, but it's delicious."

"It's calamari, sweetheart," Andrew winked.

"As long as it doesn't contain tomatoes, I'm good." I was assured by Frances that none of the courses contained tomatoes. I couldn't wait to find out what they had in store for dessert. I wasn't disappointed and the delicious concoction was just as heavenly. It was a tasty custard with a glazing of sorts atop a light pastry.

Frances greeted her guests. "I want to thank you one and all for attending and let the game begin." We were each given numbers as they were pulled from a box. It was so exciting that I had no idea who was coming or going.

When our numbers finally came up, we walked into the drawing room. We were read the rules and played our parts. Martha was thrilled that she was Miss Scarlet just like she wanted. Eleanor was miffed she was Mrs. Peacock, but she laughed it off soon enough. Strangely enough, Mr. Wilson was Colonel Mustard while Andrew was Professor Plum, and I was Mrs. White. We had fun running room-to-room making accusations with a slew of weapons from pistol to daggers.

When I walked into the library, all thoughts of the game were forgotten at the still form of Betty Lou Butler lying face down on the carpet, blood staining her lovely green gown.

Martha shrieked, as did both El and I, clinging

to each other like a lifeline. When a crowd began to pack into the room, they quickly dispersed once they spotted the dead body.

"Is this part of the game?" Mildred asked me.

"No, dear, that's a real dead body."

"Humph." She walked away like somebody who had seen a body every day of the week.

I dialed 911 and reported the crime, suggesting that everyone stay put until the police got here. Frances rushed to the doors and locked them. When the state police arrived, I would be once again face-to-face with Sheriff Peterson.

Banging on the front door had Frances rushing to let in the law. Peterson walked in with Trooper Sales and once they spotted the body, they both did a double take.

"I know, right?" I said, grimacing.

"So unexpected," El added, shrugging.

"Sure it was," Martha mocked.

While the other guests were questioned, we were in the room with the body and for the moment allowed to stay.

"Looks like a dagger was the weapon," Eleanor pointed out. "It's lying next to the body."

"Betty Lou wasn't even in our group," I informed them.

Trooper Sales rubbed his neck. "When was the last time you saw her?"

"I don't know. We were taking turns and I

hadn't noticed that she was missing at all. Until we found her body, that is."

"Fine time to notice," Peterson exclaimed. "Did you see her previously?"

"Yes, she sat one table over from us during dinner. I should have told her to watch herself."

"We went to the Butler's cemetery and we found two graves dug with the names Herman and Betty Lou carved on them," Eleanor added. "See?" She showed them the pictures on her cell phone.

Peterson's face was beet-red now. "Weren't you just in my office, Agnes? You couldn't have mentioned it then?"

I wrung my hands together. "How was I to know something bad would happen to her for sure?"

"And how exactly did you get into the cemetery, Agnes? The last I recall it's private with a locked fence," Peterson said.

"That's the strange part," I started. "The lock just fell off," I shrugged.

"How convenient," Peterson said. "And you took it upon yourselves to go onto private property without permission?"

"I'm doing a community service here. Do you want another body to turn up?"

"Of course not, Agnes, but it looks like one did. And once again another person you're investigating turns up dead!"

"I told her to tell you," El added.

I whirled with eyes flashing. "You did not, Eleanor."

"You two can quit that routine. I'm on to you," Peterson said.

"On to what, exactly?" Andrew cut in. "I was with them the whole time and none of us ever had the dagger in our hands. We were playing with plastic weapons."

"These two like to change it up to throw me off, but I'm not believing a word either of them says. East Tawas and Tadium would be a whole lot safer with the two of them locked in cold storage."

"You mean jail don't you, Peterson," I mocked his tone of voice. "That would make you not doing your job so much easier."

"I have tried to be nice to you since you saved my life and all, but it's back on."

I shook a finger in his face. "You are the poorest excuse for a sheriff that I have ever known."

"Say one more word, Agnes Barton, and the whole lot of you will be locked up."

"Under what charges, I'd like to know?" Andrew asked.

"As a lawyer you should know that I can lock anyone up for twenty-four hours."

"You do that, Sheriff, and I'll have a lawsuit on you and the sheriff's department so fast your head will spin," Andrew said. "You have no probable cause and you know it."

"You might want to listen, Peterson. This county can't afford to lose any more faith in the sheriff's department," I reminded him.

"Peterson," Trooper Sales began. "I'm disappointed at this turn in events too, but the guests are being questioned by the deputies and troopers now."

"I-I, oh my, this isn't going to be good for business, and m-my husband is going to be so angry. What if the guests want their money back?"

"Sales is right, let's all calm down. No reason to get all worked up," Peterson said. "We have a dagger that we can check for fingerprints and ... hopefully ... one of the guests will remember something."

"It's going to be like finding a needle in a haystack," I said. I then turned to Andrew. "I guess Herman Butler won't be having the cremation after all."

"That wasn't up for dispute by my client if you remember."

"Do tell me what your clients interests were?" Agnes asked.

"I'm not at liberty to discuss it. Attorney-client privilege still stands."

"Really?" Trooper Sales said. "That's most

interesting as your client may be a person of interest. Wouldn't you agree Mr. Hart?"

Andrew went to rubbing his neck and let out a sigh.

"I hope you don't plan on leaving town, Mr. Hart," Sales continued. "You know well as me that your story is suspect."

"Suspect how?"

"Since nobody in town has even seen your *client*, how do we even know you *really* even have one?" He held up his hand up silencing Andrew. "For all we know you're up to no good."

"And you're basing that on the fact I won't reveal my client's name?"

"Until we find out who is responsible for this string of murders, nobody is off the suspect list," Sales informed him.

"Have you also checked out the Butler Foundation?" I asked. "Like who the members are?"

"I have," Trooper Sales said.

"And?"

"The members of the foundation are anonymous."

"So it could be a cover or—"

"It's often a common practice with charitable organizations."

"Perhaps, but I do wonder why then would they prevent Herman Butler from being cremated?"

Sales smiled. "I guess that's a job for a senior snoop." The smile left his face as he faced Andrew again. "I sure hope you can share your client's name and soon. I hate thinking about you in this light, Andrew, but I have a job to do."

"I'm sure in a few days all of this will be cleared up."

"I certainly hope so for your sake, Mr. Hart." Sales clicked his heels and went back into the library, and a deputy led us outside.

Andrew then drove us home in silence. I had no idea what he was thinking. I only knew that he certainly had better come up with some answers and fast.

When he dropped Eleanor off, Martha and I stayed in the back seat. I avoided looking up into the mirror at all costs. My mind was racing about who could possibly want both Herman and Betty Lou dead. What about the handyman and the maid from Robinson's Manor? Had Betty Lou found out something that might have led to her death? And what about G.A.S.P.; where were they tonight? There had to be a connection... *but what was it*?

Andrew pulled into my campsite and let Martha and me out. We walked inside and as I turned to look back at Andrew, he just sat there in the LX waiting until we made it safely inside. He then left with a scattering of stones in his wake.

"This was quite a night," I said as I pulled out a box of cashew caramel clusters from the freezer, crunching into one of the frozen goodies. "If I had any alcohol I'd take a shot."

Martha went through her suitcases and took out a bottle of Jack Daniel's and I retrieved shot glasses, setting them on the table. "This certainly didn't go like I thought. Can't you folks up north just have a party without someone turning up dead?"

"Sure we can, but the police still always show up for some reason."

We clinked glasses and took the shot. I coughed a little. "I haven't had any Jack since Lord knows when."

"Me either, but after tonight it's called for."

"I wonder why Andrew just didn't reveal his client's name? Even with attorney-client privilege it seems that his client has to be on public record somewhere."

"Were papers filed at the courthouse pertaining to Andrew's client?"

"Not that I know of, unless Andrew is not sharing that information with me."

"You're not thinking that man of yours is guilty of anything, are you?"

"He's guilty all right. He has helped people in the past."

"How did that turn out?"

"He was right to protect his friend, and I know that Andrew would never do anything wrong."

"That you *know* of."

"Exactly."

"That's good because at your age it's hard to find a good man."

"I know that's the truth. Andrew can be a stubborn man at times," I agreed.

I gave Sophia a quick call and informed her about what had happened at Robinson's Manor, leaving a message on her answering machine when she didn't pick up. The whiskey had done its magic and I slowly made my way to my bed.

CHAPTER TWENTY-FOUR

I awoke the next morning and made my way toward the call of the morning coffee aroma. I poured a cup, stumbling my way to the refrigerator and poured in my vanilla creamer, filling it to the rim.

My phone rang and I answered it. "What?"

Sophia's voice crackled somewhat as she spoke. "Gramms, please come over right away."

"Okay," I said as Sophia hung up.

Martha stood like a deer in headlights. "What's up?"

"Sophia needs us to come over right away."

"Did she say why?"

"No, but we better pick Eleanor up or I'll never hear the end of it."

I called El, but she didn't pick up, and when I went over to her house, she wasn't there. Using my key, I opened the door and items were tipped over not much different than at my place the other day. My trembling hand went into my mouth and I bit down, worried what had happened to my dear friend.

"Oh my," Martha said. "There is a note here and y-you might want to read it."

I snatched it up, my eyes scanning the words scrawled across the paper. *'Bring me the money or the old lady gets it!'*

Is this real or a deliberate smokescreen? I don't have any money.

I dropped the paper and watched as it spiraled to the ground. "We better get to Sophia's place and find out what's going on. S-She d-did sound quite frantic." I dialed 911 en route to Sophia's place and reported Eleanor's disappearance. We sped over to Sophia's place and it was crawling with cops. I ran inside and Sophia hugged me tight. "Oh, Gramms, there was a break in and I was held at gunpoint! It brought so many bad memories back to me," she cried.

I pulled her away. "What were they looking for?"

"Money. The man kept insisting that you had his money and he wanted it back."

"H-He d-didn't say anything about Eleanor, did he?"

Sophia shook her head. "No, but he said before he left that she was next on his list."

"What did this man look like?"

Tears dropped to her hands and I handed her a tissue. "He was tall and thin and wore d-dark clothing and a ski mask."

I turned to Trooper Sales. "Sounds like the perp from the bank."

"He tied me up," she continued. "And if Bill hadn't shown up this morning I'd still be trussed up like a turkey."

"Why didn't you check out and see if my granddaughter was okay after what happened at Robinson's Manor last night, Sales?"

"Yeah. Why not, trooper?" Martha added. "Aren't you two hot and heavy or something?"

Bill coughed at that. "I was at the scene of the murder all night and only now made it here."

"Are you dodging my question, trooper?"

"I-I'm not sure what you mean?"

"Seriously you two just get on with it already. All of East Tawas knows besides me that the two of you are involved," I said.

"I-I'm not sure what you mean, Gramms. I told you we were just friends." Her eyes pleaded with me and I wondered in that moment if it hadn't gotten past the point of friendship, and that my loud mouth might have messed things up for her.

"Sophia is way too young for me, Agnes, and we are such good friends that I'd never betray you that way without telling you first."

Sophia began to cry uncontrollably and ran to her room. "Good move, slick," I said to him. "El is missing by the way. Her place was ransacked like mine and there was a note saying she was gonna get killed if we didn't give him the money."

Martha wrung her hands. "The note didn't say who it was, just that they wanted their money. We just assumed it might be a man with what Sophia just said." Martha then slipped inside Sophia's bedroom. I saw from the doorway Sophia was crying in her arms, telling her things that were best left to the two of them. *It's about time they caught up about things.*

"So, what now?" I asked Peterson.

"We better get over to Eleanor's house and take stock of the place."

I nodded and raced back home. I glanced about the place, but I couldn't see anywhere money could be stashed. I grabbed my Pink Lady revolver, loaded it and stuffed it in my pants pocket. I had no idea who was responsible for terrorizing Sophia and kidnapping Eleanor, but I was about to get to the bottom of it.

When I stumbled down the steps, Leotyne was standing there. "What do you want? I'm in a hurry."

"The devil has your friend," she said knowingly.

"Yes, I'm off to the Butler Mansion to get some answers."

She nodded, pressing a necklace into my trembling hands. "Just remember, if facing down pure evil, to look it in the eye and tell it to go while holding onto that stone."

I looked down at the blood-stone attached to the necklace she gave me, and then glanced up, but Leotyne was gone. I wondered how she moved so quickly, what with those long skirts and all. She must be hot as a furnace. Okay this woman freaked me out, but who knew? She might be a medium with insight into the supernatural world. At this point it made more sense to at least wear the necklace.

I raced to the Butler Mansion. It had to be a key to what was going on. That's where the crime spree first started and I hoped that's where I'd find Eleanor. Okay, so it was a hunch, but it couldn't hurt to check it out. *I, Agnes Barton, will not let anything happen to my sidekick or my granddaughter, dang it all. It's not like I could ever replace either of them.*

As I made my way toward my car, Andrew whipped in. He ran to me and took ahold of my arms. "Where are you going?"

"To find Eleanor," I answered, removing his hands from me. "Somebody took her and if I don't give them the money they are going to kill her."

"Let the police handle it."

"Like hell I will!" I moved past him.

"I'm not letting you go alone, Aggie. I love you too much to see something happen to you."

"Fine time to bring that up," I smiled. "We have to hurry." I raced to my car but he stopped me and ushered me to his vehicle instead. He then barreled toward the Butler Mansion. When we got out, the door was wide open and we made our way slowly, exchanging a look like we were of like mind.

"We should call 911," Andrew said.

"No, I think we should go in and check things out first."

He shook his head as we walked inside. I trembled as the figures carved into the woodwork of the staircase came into view. "That about scared the crap out of me," I muttered.

He nodded, equally white-faced. We walked into the kitchen, but not a thing was out of place.

Andrew took a knife from the counter. "In case we need a weapon," he whispered.

"You don't have a gun or something?"

"No."

"Well, I do." There was something about Andrew standing in the kitchen holding a knife that unnerved me. "You should put that down."

"Why?"

"Because it never works out in the movies."

"This isn't a movie, Aggie."

"I know. That's what worries me the most." I led the way up the stairs and we searched the second floor, but it was as empty as the main floor.

"We should go up to the third floor," Andrew whispered.

"You mean the one everyone falls to their death from?" I asked.

"Yes, but I have a feeling there is something we need to see up there and it would be a great place to hide somebody, possibly Eleanor."

As we continued on there was a tiny ladder with four steps that led to a door. "This must be it."

"Maybe I should go in first," Andrew suggested.

"Go ahead if you think it's easier for a man to get up there. That door is kind of small."

"I have slipped into smaller spaces than that," he winked.

I groaned at his suggestion. Or was it just my dirty mind? When he walked up there I heard a thump. I raced up the steps and as I entered the room, I saw Andrew had slumped to the floor. I knelt and turned his head toward me, my hands wet with his blood.

I bit my fist. "Oh, my."

"Oh my indeed," a voice from the corner said as a lamp lit up. Sure enough, El was gagged and tied to a chair.

I faced Teresa, the maid who stared me down, but I didn't let her intimidate me. *Is this the face of evil that Leotyne had spoken about?*

"So what gives?" I stared at her.

"What gives is that when my brother gets back, you and your friends are gonna fall out that window over there just like Mr. Butler and the handyman."

I noticed the deep groves in the floor that led to El's chair and knew how they had done it. They put that victim in the chair and simply opened the window and pushed them out. It was rigged that way. I was betting there was a mechanism on the bottom of the chair that would dump the person out quite easily. I glanced to where the maid stood and there was a chain dangling that led to the chair with a series of gears.

"Quite the setup."

"I'm glad you're impressed, Agnes. I have waited a long time for this."

"For what?"

She sneered. "For the last Butler descendant to die, but he had to go off and marry the bimbo, so she had to go, too."

"However did you orchestrate that one?"

"My brother was her date at the party. Simple, really. Robinson's Manor has secret passages and he got away easy enough in time to terrorize your granddaughter."

"And the money he demanded?"

"Clever smokescreen, don't you think? He trashed your place up pretty good to further the assumption that you had something a goon or bad guy would want."

"I did buy it at a police auction. One just never knows..."

"You're trying to be clever, aren't you?"

"Not trying, I am." I said confidently. "Did he also rob the bank?"

"He got desperate for cash. He's really an ass, but he is useful in some regards."

"And the maid that worked for Robinson's Manor."

She yawned. "I love this part best."

"What are you talking about now or should I guess? She was instructed to tell the ghost story to make everyone in town think some sort of haunting was happening. You figured that it would make it believable if a ghost really did kill Mr. Butler and the handyman, not that you'd ever convince law enforcement of that."

"You're a real know-it-all, just like Jessica Fletcher."

"I'm what you'd call a bad guy's worst nightmare." I coughed. "Your brother messed up when he killed Betty Lou. That crime just isn't going away you know."

She cackled, "You're a bit overconfident in your abilities, dear."

"So you wanted to stall the funeral just so you could finish off Betty Lou?"

"Pretty smart, but those ghost hunters made it hard to catch her unawares. The fundraiser was too good to be true. What better place for her to die then during a murder mystery at the scene of where horrific murders occurred twenty-eight years ago."

"I'm guessing your brother was in the house the day Mr. Butler took a flight out the window. He opened and closed the window to scare me."

She giggled. "It worked too."

"What about the Butler Foundation?"

"I'm the Butler Foundation. It sounds pretty official doesn't it."

"Yes, it does. Kudos for that one. But if you're the Butler Foundation, why is murdering the Butler descendants to your best interest?"

"Because if they had gotten a lawyer, they would find a loophole to take control over the foundation and the vast fortune."

"You are aware of the fact that Herman has a daughter, right?"

"That hasn't been proven yet, and before it is, she'll have an unfortunate accident."

"So you know who she is?"

"Not yet, but the lawyer there knows," she said, pointing at Andrew who still laid on the floor. "He'll tell me when I threaten to kill you."

I shook my head. "Before you actually kill me, right?"

"Of course; you must die too, along with the lawyer."

"You seem to have everything figured out. I do wonder, though..."

The door burst open and a tall thin man stepped inside. His face twisted into a sneer. "It's about time, sister dear, that we finished this."

"I'm betting she's planning to finish you," I said to the man.

"Brutus is the name. Brutus Buckerukus."

I fanned my face as if having a hot flash. "That sure is a mouthful. I hope you know that your sister here plans to kill you, too."

Brutus faced his sister. The red scar on his cheek bulged as did his eyes. "What is she talking about?"

"Don't listen to her. She's just trying to get us to turn against each other," she insisted.

"You're the perfect scapegoat and everyone has seen you, so why not blame you for all the murders. It makes perfect sense to me," I said.

His face displayed a variety of emotions. "She's right, isn't she?"

"No, she's not!"

I crept over to El while they argued and loosened her from the bindings. It was then that I heard a loud voice shout, "Grab Eleanor, she's pulling the rope!"

I grabbed El and pulled her free, but the duo

walked toward us, Brutus carrying a knife. I crept in the corner, both El and I pressed to the rafters. "Oh shit, we're gonna die!" El shouted.

The door slammed open and G.A.S.P.'s Nate and Troy raced through the door and tackled Brutus in one swoop, sending the knife whirling into the air.

Teresa picked up the knife and I stared her in the eyes like Leotyne told me and grabbed ahold of the bloodstone. This was the face of pure evil! Bright light split the room and I stepped down on something hard and metal. It sent the chair into motion and the maid fell onto it. As it sped forward it propelled her out the open window. Her screams were all we heard and then a sickening thump.

El and I raced toward the window and sure enough, the maid lay in a crumpled position below us. "Hold that man. He's a murderer," I told G.A.S.P.

Just then the police flew into the yard and troopers and deputies raced toward the house, their heavy feet pounding on the floors below us. They found their way to us within minutes. Spotlights now lit up the tiny room and I directed the police to Brutus, who Troy and Nate had restrained, informing them that he was one of the murderers they had sought and that the other could be found on the front lawn. I then knelt to Andrew who was starting to come around.

"If Andrew didn't shout out, 'Grab Eleanor, she's pulling the rope', who did?" I asked Eleanor.

"Beats me. Maybe this house really is haunted."

I walked to the wall where a portrait was hanging and in the picture was the group of senior citizens that I had seen at the first crime scene right here. "I think you might be right, El. These were the people I saw the first time we were here." I hugged El tight. "They saved you. I just know they did."

"But, Aggie," El smiled. "You don't believe in ghosts."

Tears glistened in my eyes. "I know, but I sure do now."

Nate pulled out what looked like a butchered radio. "Did you save Eleanor?"

Static came from the box and everyone froze waiting for something to happen. It became very cold, my breath like mist and a voice came from the box like a wisp of wind. "Yes."

"Did you hear that, Nate?" Jake shouted. "I knew this house was haunted!"

I smiled. "Yeah, but it's a friendly spirit."

"You mean like Casper, Aggie?"

"Nope, this one belongs to the descendants that obviously want us old folks to go on living."

Trooper Sales and Sheriff Peterson appeared and helped Andrew from the room where a stretcher waited. He was loaded and taken away as I told both Peterson and Sales what had happened and how I did my part to put it together. "How did you know to look for me here?"

"It was the scene of the first crime," Peterson said with a glint in his eye.

"Dispatch received a call from Leotyne Williams. It seems she was awful worried that Andrew and you might have run into trouble out here," Sales said. "Good thing you told her where you were going."

"She just keeps turning up and hands out the best advice."

"Premonitions that is," El added. "I believe that one has the eye."

"She sure does. I do wonder where the light came from in that room. The police hadn't arrived yet."

"Silly goose, it came from that stone you held in your hand. Didn't you see?"

"Well, no. I mean, everything happened so fast."

I turned to G.A.S.P. and asked, "Hey, how come you boys showed up?"

Nate had a smile plastered to his face. "Well, we saw you turning in here and—

"Decided to follow me or check out the mansion."

"I'm sure glad we did too or you would have been a goner for sure!"

I nodded in agreement and thanked the duo of ghost hunters.

We followed the police outside while Sales and Peterson went to check out the rigged chair. It was the closest to spy gear I had ever seen before.

We raced to the hospital and it was me waiting by Andrew's bedside for a change, not the other way around. All I knew was that he told me he loved me and I couldn't wait until I could say the same to him when he got better.

I was hugging Eleanor when Sophia and Martha rushed in the door. "I swear you two are a couple," Martha said to us.

"We sure are. A couple of super sleuths!" I then told them what happened and how we barely escaped with our lives.

EPILOGUE

Three weeks later...

I was on Hidden Cove's deck where I greeted Trooper Sales who sat next to Sophia, their fingers laced. It seems that Bill reconsidered and so did I about the whole situation. Sophia was a grown woman and quite capable of making her own decisions. I had to respect her enough to butt out as El had told me on many occasions. Not that I didn't want to do that. It was just so hard to do with Sophia. She had gone through so much and never failed to impress me with her keen ability to roll with the punches. Speaking of which, she has since taken up karate classes. Can't really blame the girl. She was going to be a lethal weapon one day and I almost felt sorry for Bill if she ever gets in a mind to toss him around. He's a bit on the short and thin side. I believe Sophia could take him quite easily. I grinned when Andrew brought me a drink. Sex on the Beach, my favorite.

"Thanks," I told Andrew. "Are you ready to give me the skinny on your mysterious client?"

"Herman Butler's daughter is Sara Knoxville."

"The actress?"

"Sure is. She wasn't known to many people as she was conceived out of wedlock. It wasn't until a few years back that Herman had met Sara."

"That must have been quite the shock."

"Yup. They had a distant relationship, but when she found out Herman had married and died mysteriously, she wanted to prevent his burial at any costs."

"I'm betting she wanted to stop the cremation."

"Sure did, but for all Betty Lou's gold digging ways, she didn't deserve to be murdered."

"I agree. I wish I'd told her that there was already a grave waiting for her."

"You didn't know she was going to be murdered."

"I know, but I still wish I had told her."

I listened in enjoyment to the friendly banter of my guests. The waves of Lake Huron lapped the shore, and I wondered if we would ever see the *Erie Board of Trade* again. It still prowls the lake and while some still consider it a myth, I know first hand it's real.

About the Author

When independent writer Madison Johns began writing at the age of forty-four, she never imagined she'd have two books in her Agnes Barton Senior Sleuths mystery series make it onto the USA Today Bestsellers list. Sure, these books are Amazon bestsellers, but USA Today?

Although sleep-deprived from working third shift, she knew if she used what she had learned while caring for senior citizens to good use, it would result in something quite unique. The Agnes Barton Senior Sleuths mystery series has forever changed Madison's life, with each of the books making it onto the Amazon bestseller's list for cozy mystery and humor.

Madison is a member of Sisters In Crime. Madison is now able to do what she loves best and work from home as a full-time writer. She has two children, a black lab, and a hilarious Jackson Chameleon to keep her company while she churns out more Agnes Barton stories with a few others brewing in the pot.

Other Books By Madison Johns

**An Agnes Barton Senior Sleuth
Mystery Series**
Armed and Outrageous
Grannies, Guns & Ghosts
Senior Snoops
Trouble in Tawas
Treasure in Tawas
Bigfoot in Tawas
High Seas Honeymoon

Agnes Barton Paranormal Mystery
Haunted Hijinks
Ghostly Hijinks
Spooky Hijinks

Kimberly Steele Romance Novella
(Sweet Romance)
Pretty and Pregnant

**An Agnes Barton/Kimberly Steele
Cozy Mystery**
Pretty, Hip & Dead

A Cajun Cooking Mystery
Target of Death

Lake Forest Witches
Meows, Magic & Murder

Kelly Gray (Stand alone) Sweet Romance
Redneck Romance

Paranormal Romance as Maddie Foxx
Clan of the Werebear
Hidden, Clan of the Werebear (Part One)
Discovered, Clan of the Werebear (Part Two)
Betrayed, Clan of the Werebear (Part Three)

Shadow Creek Shifters
Katlyn: Shadow Creek Shifters (Ménage shifter romance-Book One)
Taken: Shadow Creek Shifters (Ménage Shifter Romance) Book Two
Tessa: Shadow Creek Shifters (Vampire/Werewolf Romance)

Made in the USA
San Bernardino, CA
24 June 2016